PINKWASHED

A Novel

STARR SANDERS

Copyright © 2017 Starr Sanders
All rights reserved.

ISBN: 1539365433
ISBN 13: 9781539365433
Library of Congress Control Number: 2017901478
CreateSpace Independent Publishing Platform
North Charleston, South Carolina

DEDICATED

to

My granddaughters, Leah and Sage, my hope for the
future to make a difference in this world

and

Andy Silverman, my loving partner and best friend
who has never stopped making a difference.

Chapter One

The true name of the town where this story takes place isn't really important. What's important is that it's a small American city in a flyover state, the kind of place that's politically irrelevant until suddenly it isn't. What's also important is this is a true story, that it's mine to tell, and that I paid a price for speaking my mind. And here I sit in jail, awaiting trial.

Let's say my city is called Greenville, because to tell the story I'll need to call it something. I've changed everybody's names, too, as well as the names of the companies and organizations mixed up in the whole debacle.

I was a member of the Greenville City Council, elected to represent the public by my voters. There were twenty thousand two hundred and five constituents in my district and roughly a hundred thousand in the city limits. Like I said, Greenville isn't a big place. But little cities like ours are places where the social landscape begins its inevitable changes, albeit at glacier speed, where the attitudes of the heartland start to shift. Out on the coasts, you can count on a certain level of liberal thought. Not here in the middle, yet.

I'm a Democrat, a centrist one, pretty standard, at least publicly. Riding the middle is the only way to stay in office in a place like this. I am secretly more liberal than I admit in public and hopeful that positive change always happens sooner or later. Given everything I know about my neighbors and my constituents, the current progressive wave carrying gay marriage and legal marijuana won't be lapping up to these landlocked parts for a while yet. When it does, the residents of Greenville will dip their toes into the water of reason and kindness and realize how good it feels to be on the right side of history.

And, when that happens – poof! - history changes! This is why I loved my job.

As I saw it, my job was to identify systemic problems and fix them according to the will of the people. I took it seriously which, I suppose, is what got me arrested and landed me in jail. Normally, white-collar criminals like me await trial in the comfort of their homes.

Also, I have breast cancer. I'm nearly done with the chemotherapy - ten treatments in all. I was diagnosed when my recent campaign was in full swing and my advisors determined it would be bad strategy to announce it. So, during most months of my campaign, I wore a wig and glasses to Greenville General Hospital for my surgery and chemo visits.

The cancer is how this all started - how the whole wild story began. The cancer is what opened my eyes. I saw things I'd never seen before. And please, let me be clear: I am not one of those people who will try to tell you that *cancer is a gift.* That's crazy talk and we all know it. Not that I could ever be this honest in public, but nobody is ever going to read this story. I'm writing it all down just to keep myself from going crazy in this place. In this jail.

My god, the things I couldn't say in public would fill the heavens. And when it all eventually came out— that I had cancer, that I'd committed fraud—I did, I'm ashamed to admit, utter a few of those clichés for the cameras. *The cancer taught me every day is precious. The cancer brought me closer to my loved ones.* All of which is true, of course, which I guess is why clichés are so popular.

What I mean by the cancer opening my eyes is that it made me fearless. I dodged a bullet – and walking around with that feeling is a powerful drug. More directly, my eyes were opened because I started hanging out at the hospital. I have been blessed all my life with decent health so I've never spent much time in one. I'm a person who keeps her eyes open to what I see around me. I started to see the healthcare system in a new way, and it started to piss me off.

I was angry already, of course. You can't be a decent elected official if you aren't a little bit pissed off all the time. I mean, the shit that lands on your desk just makes you want to spend the day crying: evicted families, deported children, dead homeless people, dried up aquifers. The bad news just keeps coming. And it's our job to look deeper than the bad news, to the rotten core of things, in order to fix them. To ask questions. Which means spending a lot of time studying the rotten core. Which is bound to keep you at least a little bit pissed off. Because it stinks down there.

And I suppose being a little bit pissed off all the time does improve your chances of eventually getting cancer. Anger gnaws at you. I learned this seven years ago, when I got divorced. I held onto that anger for a long time and it did me no good.

Still, I knew what I'd signed on for. Politics isn't exactly a low-stress job. I knew the gig involved long hours and big anxiety and lousy food, but I didn't figure it would give me cancer, for chrissake. It's as if my body was absorbing the toxic fumes rising off the rotten core I'd been studying so hard. Talk about a sacrifice for the common good. You look hard at evil, to study it so you can kill it, and instead you inhale its off-gasses and it begins eating you from the inside out.

Not that I have any reason to complain. My cancer didn't kill me and probably won't. But my campaign advisors determined I shouldn't announce the cancer until after the election, despite my positive prognosis, and the reason was the type of breast cancer I ended up with. It's an extremely rare form called Paget's disease—and it's a cancer of the nipple.

"Seriously, Peg?" said July, my campaign manager, the afternoon I gathered them all in the conference room. We were nearly three months away from Election Day. "The nipple?"

The room was full of staffers. In addition to July, there was Dan the media guy; Manuel the expensive strategy consultant; my new executive assistant whose name I couldn't remember; the volunteer coordinator; and two interns. Normally the candidate's cancer diagnosis isn't the kind of thing you share with interns, but we needed bodies to run interference with the hospital and the media. Plus, this wasn't exactly Chicago: the entire campaign budget was just shy of fifty thousand dollars. Manuel was the only one making a salary; everyone else was volunteering or being criminally underpaid. Interns did a lot of technical stuff that was, practically, beyond their abilities.

"Nipple," muttered the media guy, Dan, frowning at his notepad. "Nipple. That's going to be a tough story to twist."

Jennifer burst into snorts of laughter. "Sorry," she said.

Jennifer is my niece as well as a campaign intern. She had already been told about my diagnosis; I went to my sister's place for dinner the night before to break the news. After some crying, we all eventually indulged in a cleansing and prolonged family laugh over the absurdity of nipple cancer. Today, though, poor Dan was turning shades of red. He hadn't had time to develop a sense of humor about it. Nobody in the room had enough time. There we were, Jennifer and me, shaking with laughter in a room full of our shocked and silent colleagues.

They waited politely as we worked our faces back to normal. Certainly they were thinking about the election, which was coming soon. We'd been doing everything possible to prevent a surprise smear campaign we knew would be coming from the opposition.

My chemo treatments were to start the next day.

"If they're going to expose you as having cancer," July said, "they'll need to do it soon. And even if they did, they'd need to work pretty hard to turn the most sympathetic disease in America into a reason not to vote for you. If the truth comes out, we'll release a statement about your desire for privacy and they'll look like fools."

She was right. Still, that didn't mean I was ready for the whole city to focus its attention on my left nipple. "Plus the prognosis is good," I said. "It's not a life threatening situation at all. As cancers go, it's a little wimpy, to tell you the truth. I'll need surgery. They'll need to remove the actual nipple in question, I'm afraid, and then they'll do reconstruction as best they can, which as it turns out actually isn't very good," and now I was on a roll, telling them things they didn't need to know. "Apparently medical science hasn't really caught up to nipple reconstruction. That's a bummer, of course, but I understand there's some hipster tattoo artist in Brooklyn who does a really great job with nipple stimulation, so there's hope yet."

I took a breath, saw their puzzled and contorted faces, realized what I'd just said. "Simulation! I meant *simulation.*"

"Anyway," Jennifer interjected, after another awkward pause.

"Right, anyway," I said. "Surgery and chemo. So if we're going to keep this on the *down low,*" here I checked Jennifer's face for confirmation I'd used the term correctly and found her cringe more loving than mortified. "We'll need a plan." I asked the team for their thoughts and sat back in my chair.

I was exhausted already and hadn't even started chemo yet. For the first time in years I was sorry my

Chapter Two

I've been in jail 47 days. Fifteen left to go before my trial.

My cellmate is a nineteen-year-old girl named Mercedes who got caught breaking into houses one too many times. The last time she had a switchblade on her, which upped her possible sentence to five years. She told me on my first day in the cell that she didn't want to be a meth whore so instead she stole stuff. Mercedes' mother died two years ago and basically her life went to shit. I'm 50, childless and with a raging maternal instinct. So you can guess where this is leading. I'm doing my best not to mother this girl but she's utterly lost.

This is what you get in the county lockup. Fallen politicians accused of computer fraud sharing quarters with drug addicts accused of theft. Really, there's not much difference between people. We're all pretty much the same.

Mercedes talks a lot. She's in the middle of a rambling story about some bitch back in high school who threatened her in the girls' bathroom with a sharpened hair clip. Because there's nothing whatsoever to do in jail, I'm actually listening, asking for details. What kind of makeup was the bitch wearing? Did she bring her friends with her? When the guard shows up to tell me I have a visitor, I experience a weird reluctance to leave our cell. Lockup must be getting to me.

My visitor is July, my oddly-named, former campaign manager. She sits at one of the tables in the visiting room with a look of professional blankness on her face. July is a pretty woman: twenty-five, thick black hair, perfect skin, eyes like a Disney princess. The kind of woman a 50-year old candidate with an ass the size of mine and a face that's sinking fast really doesn't want at her side. When July walked into my office for the job interview six months ago, my first thought was that working with this woman would be like every single day putting on a dress that makes you look fat. Yet she turned out to be ridiculously qualified and, let's be honest, beautiful people get what they want more often than the rest of us.

I figured she'd be an asset to the campaign but July ended up screwing me over. Why are we always surprised when beautiful people turn out to be manipulative assholes?

I sit down across from her in the plastic chair attached to the table. In the last 47 days I've spent time in prisoner visiting rooms and have noticed the chairs are always attached either to the table or the floor. Now, sitting across from July the Traitor, I understand why. If the furniture wasn't bolted down, I'd be tempted to swing my chair at her head with serious malicious intent. She's the reason I'm in here.

"You probably don't want to see me," July says.

I lean back in my chair, cross my arms over my chest in imitation of a hardened criminal. "Not at all. It's always a delight," I say back, stone-faced.

July is wearing a raw silk blouse of the palest pink. She is so idiotically beautiful that she makes even that awful color look pretty. She knows about my pink aversion and wearing it is a low blow on her part.

This whole nasty business began back in September, well over a month before Breast Cancer Industry Month in October. Under its mainstream guise as Breast Cancer Awareness Month, it makes itself known all across America through the aggressive use of the color pink.

I hate pink. I've always hated pink. I hate it in all its forms. From dusty rose to Pepto Bismol, from baby-blanket pastel to fuck-me fuchsia, I despise the color and have always refused to wear it. As a female politician, this is not an easy row to hoe. They're always trying to force it on you. All this pink has made my visits to Greenville General Hospital for chemo treatments particularly irritating.

The Sharon T. Boland Foundation, the national nonprofit research conglomerate that raises buckets of money for breast cancer research, had developed a partnership with the hospital which, as far as I could see, consisted mainly of transforming any available surface or wall into an opportunity for more pink.

If I thought the hospital was bad, the shopping mall was worse. From The Gap to the NFL, the commercialization of breast cancer was unsettling even before I became one of its victims. Now that I actually have it, evidence of every corporation in America sucking on the pink marketing teat was doubly offensive.

"Nice shirt," I said to July. It was a thing we used to say, sort of a bitter tag line. We'd all gather to watch our opponent on TV, being a jerk or a liar or just plain incompetent and sooner or later someone would say, *Well, at least he's wearing a nice shirt.* It was almost always true. Our opponent was, indeed, a snappy dresser.

"Oh god," she said, looking down at herself. "Shit, I'm sorry."

"Nice to hear," I snap back.

"What?" July says. "That I'm sorry? Well, I am. I've told you so. That's why I came. I'm here to tell you again."

At my bail hearing I was ordered to cut all contact with July. But I didn't. When they let me out on bail, I went to visit her at her house. I was busted, and that's why I'm awaiting trial in jail rather than in the comfort of my home.

The judge basically expected me to sit quietly, awaiting my doom, when it was still very possible to gather information that would exonerate me. When I went to her house that night, a reporter followed me and took a picture. That little slip-up landed me back in court, where the district attorney painted me as a losing candidate, obsessed to an unhealthy degree with Regional Oil, Incorporated. He said I had a vendetta. He called me a vigilante. The guy's a supreme asshole.

The terms of my release pending trial were equivalent to a restraining order. I was to stay at least 100 feet away from July at all times. A particularly vindictive judge—a law school buddy of my campaign opponent—heard the case. Despite my cancer and even despite the chemo, he sent me to jail for the remaining weeks before my trial.

In the meantime, local reporters and bloggers were seizing upon the seedy familiarity of restraining order language —the vocabulary of stalking, of crazy person violence—and repeating it again and again. All I did was knock on July's door. All we did was sit in her living room and have a conversation. The coverage of the scandal had been deeply embarrassing, to say the least. The papers were now painting me as that crazy politician who snapped and went completely bonkers.

"You showed up to say you're sorry?" I ask July. "A postcard would've done fine."

She adjusts her blazer in an attempt to cover the offending pinkness below it. "Actually," she says, "there's another thing." I grunt in satisfaction. July can manipulate situations better than almost anyone I know. Almost as well as me. I wonder what she wants.

"The fan club," she says.

"Oh Lord," I say.

The fan club is shorthand for the wild-eyed crazies who haven't abandoned me yet. These are my hardcore campaign volunteers; the kind of people who attach to a candidate in a way that's way too emotional for their own good.

Politics brings out these types in droves. They're worshippers in need of an idol. Fan clubbers will love you no matter what you do and are the kind who fall to emotional bits in the face of an impending loss. They cannot let go. They refuse to believe I'm in the wrong. For their blind faith in me, I love them unreasonably.

My fan club is made up of a group of 20 or 30 people, mostly retirees, who spent the last six months stuffing envelopes, making sandwiches, raising money, and knocking on every door in my district. They are lovely people who are dedicated to democracy and are too stupid or courageous to abandon their candidate, even when she's awaiting trial on charges of fraud. To anyone with a shred of common sense, I'm political poison. Yet to the fan club, I'm a martyr.

Still, besides my family and my untrustworthy former campaign manager, the fan club is all the community I've got left.

"They're planning to walk as a group in your honor for the Sharon T. Boland Run for Cancer Research."

"Oh, please, no," I say.

"They've made T-shirts."

"You're killing me, July. Could you go home now? Please? My cellmate was in the middle of a really great story about this time back in high school—"

"The race is in two weeks," July says, "the day before your trial begins."

"Tell them to back off," I say. "They can't do this. Seriously!" If the fan club knew how the Boland Foundation was mixed up in all this, they'd certainly want nothing to do with that damn race.

"I think you should support them," July says. "You need the PR."

I stared at her openmouthed, in the way Mercedes gapes at me in disbelief when I tell her details of my last year. Even though she talks a lot, Mercedes can be a good listener. Funny how I'm taking on her facial expressions already.

Then it registers: what July wants. "Why do you care that I need the PR?" I ask.

"If you're convicted of fraud, nobody gains," she says.

"How's your career, July?" I ask. "Where are you working now? Did you take that offer at Welles and Steinberg?"

July looks at her knuckles, which are white. "They rescinded it," she says.

"Aha," I say. "So the stink of my malfeasance clings to you, does it?"

She raises her head and looks me directly in the eye. "In fact, yes. It does. I'm virtually unemployable."

"The whistleblower strategy didn't quite cover you, I take it?"

"Too little, too late," she says. "The thinking was that I should have come forward sooner. Way sooner." She glances around the room, lowers her voice. "Before I actually…"

"Participated?" I say.

"Before I played the role that I did," she says. "Listen." She leans forward and speaks in a whisper. "We both know our motives were pure. We both know we had good reason. We uncovered serious shit and we were backed up against the wall. The election was approaching. We had to do something."

This surprises me: July's admission of fault and her continued solidarity with the cause, if not with me. I sit back in my chair.

"What did you expect, Peg?" July says. "I have family. I have a career. I know this is your life but for me it was just a job. Once I saw there was no way to get away with what we'd started, I had to go to the elections board."

"And you had to tell them I coerced you," I say.

"My attorney insisted," July tells me. "She said it was the only way. I fought her on it. I fought everybody on it. I told them it wasn't right for you to take the blame alone."

"Anyway," I say. "Go on. The fan club."

"Good PR," she repeats. "The Boland Cancer Run."

"And what happens when it all comes out that I was trying to expose the Boland Foundation? And it's reported that my supporters were all up in that damn race, wearing t-shirts with my face on them?"

"We'll worry about that after you're acquitted. Right now we need public sympathy and this is how to get it. The staff agrees."

"The staff?" I say. "Whose staff?"

"Yours, of course," she says.

"Mine?" I repeat dumbly. Everyone lost their jobs when I was tossed in the slammer, of course.

"We met last night," July says. "At my place. Everybody agrees, Peg. Everybody knows you did what had to be done."

I am stunned. I thought they all hated me. "I broke the law," I say, tears welling, aching in gratitude for such loyalty.

"Sometimes," July says, reaching to lay her hand on my arm, "the law is asking for it."

Chapter Three

Greenville was built on the oil business. Our largest employer is Regional Oil, Inc., the company for which my father and grandfather worked as roughnecks their entire lives.

My ex-husband hated Regional Oil. He said it was wrecking Greenville and my father and brother were just ignorant cogs in the machine of global warming. My brother Billy took up the family tradition about five years ago and worked his way quickly up the food chain to tool pusher, the guy who lives at the rig for weeks at a time and bears ultimate responsibility for the crew.

It was Billy who first told me about the breast cancer drill bits.

We were at his daughter's third birthday party, less than five weeks before the election. My niece is a damn cute three-year-old, a genre of human that I find uniformly adorable. July had generously scheduled me a twenty-minute drive-by, squeezing the party in-between a fundraising coffee and a visit to the municipal dump to shake the hands of sanitation workers.

I was determined to refrain from giving Billy a hard time about the preponderance of princess paraphernalia at his kid's party. Soon enough, though, he caught me at the food table, frowning at his wife's decorating job: pink frosting, pink streamers, pink napkins, lavender balloons.

"I knew you'd love this," he said.

"It's like we're inside the vagina of the sugar plum fairy," I told him.

Billy smiled, shrugged his shoulders, took a gulp out of his big plastic cup of beer and looked sideways at me, his eyes gleaming.

"What?" I asked. "Spill it."

He was clearly holding onto some news. As my barely younger brother, my Irish twin, one of his lifelong pleasures was to work me into a lather over social injustice. When we were kids, he told me tales of thoughtless teachers, cruel schoolyard behaviors, and dictatorial parents. I wonder sometimes whether it was Billy's habit of firing me up about the small unfair moments of life that led to my career in politics. All those years, he was my primary audience as I tested out my young and passionate thoughts on second-wave feminism, ecology, and the war in Iraq.

And he fought with me over all of it. For Billy, debate has always been a sport. Maybe it was all those years of arguing the other side that turned him into a Republican. Or maybe it was just because, like the rest of our family, he really held those values.

As the family's only Democrat, I was the black sheep. In any case, having grown up to become a professional guardian of leftist social justice and a publicly-endorsed loudmouth, I remained an attractive audience for Billy's tales of institutionalized discrimination, corporate greed, and legislative tomfoolery.

"So, a shipment of new drill bits comes into the rig last week," Billy said, grinning into his big plastic cup of Miller Lite. "And they're pink."

"Pink drill bits?" I asked. As the daughter of a rigger I know what a drill bit looks like - kind of a phallic cyborg arm the diameter of a dinner plate, shaped at the fist like a cardinal's hat and embedded with dozens of spinning wheel blades. For some reason—industrial superstition, no doubt—they're normally painted gold.

Billy had that gleam in his eye. It had been a while since he'd had the joy of being the first person to tell me about some new outrage. "It's a breast cancer thing," he said, no longer even trying to suppress his glee. "Each one comes packaged with educational information, including those cards you hang in the shower that tell you how to do a breast self-exam."

"Oh my god," I murmur.

"Yeah, the guys on the rig are super interested. Everybody's totally well-informed now. By the way, sis, are you getting regular mammograms?"

"Shut up," I told him. Billy didn't know yet about my diagnosis. Now seemed the wrong time to tell him.

He pulled his phone out of his pocket and showed me a picture. His crew was gathered in goofy poses around a newly installed hot pink drill.

"Let me guess. Does this have anything to do with The Sharon T. Boland Foundation?" I pulled out my phone and googled BOLAND PINK DRILL BIT.

"Yeah. The company gave them a hundred thousand bucks."

My search results came up empty. "Nothing," I told him.

"They haven't made the announcement yet. There was a photographer there, getting shots of the guys thoughtfully and respectfully installing the thing. She got them to say stuff about the breast health of their mothers and daughters. They could hardly talk without busting out in laughter."

"I cannot believe this is real," I said, looking again at the photo on his phone. But I was staring right at it: a picture of an absurd fuchsia industrial drill bit. I looked up at him. "Tell me this is a joke."

"I'm as flabbergasted as you are, sis," Billy said. "I mean, seriously, it's the most insane thing. Apparently, they made a thousand of them."

"What were the company's revenues last year?" I asked Billy. "Like twenty billion dollars?"

"Give or take," he said.

"And for a measly hundred grand they get to pinkwash their bullshit?"

"Whatwash?" Billy said.

"It's a fracking bit," I said. "Right?"

"Not this again," he said.

"Yes, this again. Benzene again. You know, that carcinogen you and your guys are pumping into the ground every day? The shit that's making our tap water burst into flames?"

"That only happened like twice—" he protested.

"The shit you're breathing into your lungs?" I continued. "The shit that puts you and your crew at a thousand times greater risk for leukemia?"

"Nobody's proven that—"

"Don't be dense, Billy. Of course they've proven it. And what's more, what's worse, what's so fucking outrageous about what I'm seeing here," as I waved my phone in his face, "is that benzene is linked to breast cancer."

"Pretty ballsy of the old company, I gotta say. We've got some evil geniuses in the marketing division," Billy said.

"For a tiny fraction of a tinier fraction of their annual profits, Regional Oil gets public credit for giving a rat's ass about women. A hundred grand? Less than the company spends on toilet paper."

"I dunno," Billy replied. "Roughnecks do go through a lot of TP."

"Yeah, well, they'll be using a lot more of it when the leukemia starts melting their insides," I said, knowing I wasn't making any sense but too pissed off to care.

I pulled up the Boland Foundation's website on my phone. I had to see the names of the dimwits who approved this idea. "This is the most egregious piece of pink bullshit I've ever seen. Hiding the enemy under their girly skirts!" I wailed. "Where do they get the gall?"

I navigated to the webpage that listed their board of directors.

"What?" Billy was saying. "Oh my god, stop smiling like that. You'll frighten the children."

I couldn't help it. I'd just been handed a delightful political gift. There it was, on the Boland Foundation's website. The chair of their board was Helene Boswell.

I whispered her name reverently, thanking God for this stroke of good fortune.

"Who's that?" Billy asked.

"My opponent's wife," I told him.

"No kidding," Billy said, as a gang of toddlers came running full tilt into the living room. Judging from the eagerness in their eyes, they'd been promised cake. Right this moment, I knew exactly how they felt.

"Well done, bro," I said, pocketing my phone looking around for my coat. I kissed the adorable birthday girl and dug into my purse for my car keys. "Thanks to you, we've got our October election surprise."

Chapter Four

I guess I'll never know how the media managed to miss the connection between Helene Boswell and the fracking industry. The decline of real newspapers, I suppose. For a hundred years Greenville was a two-newspaper city: *The Star* in the morning and *The Sun* in the evening.

Last year *The Sun* was swallowed whole by a multi-media conglomerate out of Dallas, which shut it down as unprofitable eight months after the purchase. This leaves us with *The Star*, which was always the lesser quality of the two, favoring crosswords and comics and classifieds over hard news. Their politics reporter also covered sports, arts, and weather.

In this particular case, though, the slow death of journalism in Greenville worked in our favor. Now we could control the release of this news. Our angle with the press would be that as chair of the Boland board, my opponent's wife was technically and legally the person to be held accountable for the drill bit gambit.

In Greenville, the Boland Foundation board was a prestige post, akin to the symphony and the art museum. If fracking weren't such a hot button issue this campaign season, Helene Boswell's life as a socialite volunteer would be irrelevant. The Boland board members were the original Ladies Who Lunch, the Junior Leaguers, and the DAR set. They lived in homes bordering the golf course and were married to members of what we in politics euphemistically call "the business community." If it weren't for fracking, Helene Boswell spending her time raising money for breast cancer research wouldn't be a campaign issue at all except as a feather in her husband's cap.

But her husband, my opponent, had been dancing around fracking for the last nine months. Even in this generally conservative city, Regional Oil and the industry in general were having an increasingly hard time defending themselves. Just last week, a hundred activists dressed in green turned up at the city council hearing regarding the possible awarding of another oil field permit. Their presence clearly rattled Boswell, my opponent. As a businessman, Boswell attended these hearings and by all accounts was ready to voice his approval for the permit. But when his turn came, he encouraged the council to table the decision for further study.

Billy was right that the flammable water incidents were, in fact, rare. Yet as the Ebola hysteria has taught us, when the images are scary enough, rare is all you need. My opponent was a longtime, steadfast supporter of Regional Oil, having himself been an executive there for much of his career. And just before he announced his candidacy last year, he sold his stock in the company and since has been doing all he can to distance himself.

As Hollywood and social media increasingly condemn fracking as the evil it is, politicians who defend the practice find creative ways to walk the line between the business community—their biggest campaign donors—and an increasingly suspicious electorate. My opponent's position paper on fracking concedes it's "an imperfect solution" but reducing our dependence on foreign oil is of greater national priority. The position paper neglects to acknowledge that he's running for city council, not Congress, and therefore the promotion of national priorities falls entirely outside his job description. But he's skating on thin ice and he knows it.

The morning after the birthday party at Billy's, I gathered the brain trust in my office to discuss how we might do the most damage with this information.

"So, why would his wife be okay with this drill bit business?" July pondered. "It's poison for her husband's campaign."

"Not to mention for the drinking water," said Dan, the media guy.

"They probably assumed nobody would care, nobody would notice," said Jennifer.

July looked at Jennifer with an expression that wasn't hard to read. She believed interns should be seen and not heard. And she was right. If Jennifer weren't my niece, she'd be fetching us coffee and certainly not sharing her opinions.

"No," I said. "My brother says they're preparing a press release. They think this is a good idea. They're off their rockers."

"Maybe this is why Boswell looked so scared at the council hearing last week, when all those protestors showed up," Jennifer said. "Why he backed off his vote. He knew Regional Oil was about to unveil the drill bits."

We all stopped to consider this. My niece is a pretty bright kid.

"Well, let's frame it our way before they get the chance," July said. "We've got to get our press release over to *The Star* today." She'd been sketching out possible headlines. How about this. *Candidate's Wife Caught in Bed with Regional Oil."*

We all turned to her and stared.

"What?" she said. "Too much?"

"A little misogynistic, don't you think?" Jennifer said. "And not very impartial, for a news headline."

"We don't need to be impartial, honey," I said. "That's the newspaper's job. Our job is to frame the debate. To offer a perspective they might adopt, language they might use." I eyed July. "Without making us look sleazy."

"C'mon, Dan," July said, smirking. "Let's go craft a tattle-tale press release that takes the high road."

But fifteen minutes later July was back in my office, Dan at her heels. She was on the phone with the reporter from *The Sun.* "Yes, of course, Janice," she was saying into her phone as she burst through the door. "The philanthropic relationship between Boland and Regional Oil has always been public knowledge. And yes, yes, Helene Boswell's role at Boland is public knowledge, too. What's different this time," she said, rolling her eyes at me as she frantically spun the story, "is that now she's the candidate's wife. And that a candidate's wife is helping a fracking company lie to the citizenry—"

She stopped talking, nodding her head, then shaking it, a politico working her phone. "Sure it's a lie!" she said. "Because benzene, that's why—"

Interrupted again, she met my eye and slapped her forehead to communicate the unimaginable idiocy of her conversation. "Yes," she said. "Okay, fine. Yes. There's always social media, yes, indeed. Okay, then. Right."

She put her phone in her pocket. "She says it's nothing new. They won't write a piece. She says if we think it's so important we should put it on Twitter."

"Which we sure as hell will," Dan said. "It's not as if we need print media anymore."

"Yes, sure, let's tweet it but something's going on here," I said. "This is as newsworthy as anything that's happened in this campaign so far, and fracking is the hottest button issue of the year. Yet *The Star* won't publish it. What're they scared of?"

We all stood there frowning at one another.

Jennifer poked her head into the office. "Uncle Billy's on the phone," she told me. "He said I should interrupt you."

I waved July and Dan back to their offices and picked up the phone.

"What the fuck, Peggy," Billy said.

"Clarify?" I replied.

"What have you done? I just got called into the executive office. They tore my head off."

"What? Why?"

"The drill bits. The goddamn pink drill bits. What did you go and do now?"

"Wow," I said. "What did they want? What did they say?"

"What did they say?" I could practically hear the veins on Billy's neck popping out. "This is what you ask me? You don't ask if I'm okay? If I still have my job?"

"Oh my god, Billy, did they fire you?"

"Just about."

"But why? Because of my press release?"

"Okay. Okay. Okay." Billy was doing that panting thing he did when he was upset.

"Sit down, Billy," I told him. "Is there a paper bag handy?"

"Shut the fuck up," he said, panting. "A press release? You wrote a press release? What were you thinking?"

"I was thinking I'd scoop them, that's what. I was thinking I'd expose the madness before they had a chance to spin it as some kind of sick philanthropy."

"You weren't thinking about me, that's for damn sure," Billy said.

"What did they say?"

I heard Billy's palm covering his phone. His voice, muffled, telling someone he'd be right there.

"Where are you?" I asked when he came back on the line.

"On the rig," he said. "Just shut up for a minute, okay?"

"Right," I said.

"So they told me I needed to rein you in."

"You?" I sputtered. "You need to *rein me in?* What century are these guys living in?"

"Please, Peg. Please just shut up."

"Sorry. Go on."

"They're scrapping the whole thing," he said. "We've been ordered to put the pink bits back in the crates and pretend it never happened. Apparently, they got a call from the newspaper about half an hour ago. Reporter asking about benzene, about formaldehyde, about breast cancer. The reporter mentions your name, mentions Helene Boswell."

"Wow," I said. "So *The Sun* called them after all. This is so classic. They're scared."

"Whatever," Billy said. "The bottom line is my job is in jeopardy because I showed you that picture. Not that they know that. But they put the pieces together quick enough. Next time you run for office, how about doing me a favor and changing your name."

"They're using you," I said. "You realize that, right? They're using you to deliver a message." A thought struck me. "Send me the photo, Billy," I said. "Please."

"Are you fucking kidding me? Haven't you been listening?"

"If they ditch the whole program, we've got nothing," I told him. "There's no story. We can't use the pinkwash."

"Tough shit, sis," Billy said. "You should've thought of that before you tried to screw my employer. The company that feeds my kids. No way am I sending you anything. Sorry to wreck your October ambush."

"Surprise," I corrected him. "October surprise."

"Yeah, well. Boo. Surprise," he said, and hung up.

Chapter Five

My cellmate Mercedes is of the opinion that I should have sneaked into my brother's home and stolen his mobile phone. We are deep into a conversation about my legal defense, off on a tangent about what landed me here. I spend many hours a day with this girl. I'd already filled her in on my disastrous marriage, my inability to have children, and the nipple tattoo plan. Certain barriers have been broken, shall we say.

"If you'd stolen his phone though, you'd have gotten the photo, aren't I right?" she states. "You'd have sent it to the reporter and the story would have been in the paper and you'd have won the election fair and square and none of this other bullshit would have happened."

"The trouble with you, Mercedes, is that you think stealing is a valid strategy."

"You're not exactly one to talk, dude," she informed me.

"Point taken," I say. If only I'd known back in October that those drill bits were only the tip of the pink iceberg.

"But anyway," I continue, "it turned out that our press release is what started the chain of events." Later, my guy, Manuel, informed me how stupid it was to try to get out ahead of the story. "We should have waited for them to announce the partnership and then reacted with indignation," Manuel said. Which, presumably, he would have advised me, had he been picking up his phone that day and not on his way to Washington, DC to interview for a job with a congressman from a different state.

"What happened next?" Mercedes asks.

"We got to see their reaction," I tell her. "It was so intense, so over the top. Why would they threaten my brother? It didn't make sense. So we started looking harder at the whole thing. What kind of arrogant corporate executive thinks it makes sense to pressure an employee to influence a politician in the family?"

"A bunch of white dudes, that's who," Mercedes says.

"White ladies, actually," I say. "The CEO of Regional Oil is a woman. And so is the CFO and about a dozen vice presidents."

"Oh yeah, I think I knew that," Mercedes says.

"Astonishing, isn't it?"

"My grandma used to tell me stories about those ladies."

Mercedes' grandmother is a janitor at Regional Oil. I learned this on the second day of my incarceration. It's the one thing Mercedes and I have in common. We're the granddaughters of company employees. The coincidence is not entirely unexpected, given the company is the biggest employer in Greenville, but a nice convergence, nonetheless. Mercedes seems comforted by our shared experience.

"Why would your grandma talk to you about female executives?" I ask.

"Why wouldn't she?" Mercedes replied, with an indignant edge to her voice.

"No, sorry, I meant what did her job have to do with them?"

"You mean, why should the cleaning lady concern herself with the people who are running the company?"

"Mercedes, give me a break," I said. "You know I'm not a racist, so cut it out."

"Everybody's a racist."

"Okay, what I mean is that for a middle-aged white person, I'm not so racist. What did your grandma tell you about the ladies at the company?"

"That they made messes," she said. She launches into her impression of her grandmother, a voice into which she lapses so often and so effectively that it's as if a sixty-eight-year-old lady from Juarez was always poised to spring from the girl's body. "They don't throw cups in the garbage can that's sitting right there!" Mercedes yelled. "They don't flush their bloody tampons! The locker room stinks and they pee in the showers!"

Mercedes. This girl cracks me up. "So, what happened next," I told her, "is that we started to wonder what they were trying to say by threatening Billy. And we thought about how weird it was that they'd even do that. How extreme. It was as if they were scared of something."

"I mean, did they think you'd just back off? That you wouldn't start poking around, trying to find out what they were hiding?"

"Exactly!" I said.

"I told my grandma about you," Mercedes said. "She says you shouldn't have hacked into that guy's computer but she likes you anyway."

"How sweet," I said. Mercedes holds her grandmother in incredibly high esteem. In the deep of night when she sobs in the upper bunk over the terrible choices she made and the people she's hurt or disappointed, her grandmother is the person over whom she cries the hardest.

"She hates working at that place," Mercedes told me. "She says they're all crooks and liars. She speaks good English but she pretends she doesn't. She says it's safer in places like that to play dumb."

"It sounds like she works hard," I said.

"Want to meet her?" Mercedes says. "She's coming tomorrow, to see me. You could say hello."

"Oh, honey, you should have your time alone with your grandma. I don't want to impose." Besides, I was looking forward to an hour alone.

"Sure, ok," she said. "But sometime you've got to meet her. Okay?"

"Right," I said. I punch my pillow and tell Mercedes I'm going to take a nap.

"I'll shut up, then," she said amiably.

I closed my eyes and as I was falling asleep an image of my ex-husband appeared to me, as clear as day. He was wearing a ruffled tuxedo shirt and a bow tie dangled from his neck. We were on the beach in Santa Monica after my sister's wedding. He was smiling at me and calling my name. Shirtsleeves were rolled up. His forearms were muscled and tan.

And then, the magic half-alert portion of my brain activated itself in the space between sleep and waking. I thought of Mercedes' grandmother cleaning up the locker room at Regional Oil - the executives' locker room.

A Hispanic lady cleaning the toilets and emptying the garbage. A woman who seems not to speak English. The kind of non-person in front of whom corporate executives tend to speak freely.

"Mercedes?"

"Yeah?"

"Maybe I'll come meet your grandma after all."

Chapter Six

My staff started digging into why Regional Oil reacted so strongly to our press release about the drill bits. We assumed Boswell had applied pressure to the company to avoid attention to his pro-fracking position, but if he was so concerned, why hadn't he stopped the project before it got this far? Presumably he'd have known months earlier about the sponsorship collaboration between Regional Oil and the Boland Foundation. Surely, his wife would have told him. This is the kind of thing the charity chairwoman of Boland definitely mentions to her husband, a former Regional Oil executive. This is the kind of idea that, in any normal political marriage, gets discussed, chewed over and run through the campaign advisors.

Maybe the Boswell marriage wasn't as happy as it seemed. I knew as much as anyone about keeping up appearances even when your marriage is failing. Maybe Helene Boswell was trying to sabotage her husband's campaign. The woman did, in fact, have a vacant, emotionally-disassociated look about her.

On the way to the hospital I floated this idea past July. She was driving, with Jennifer and Dan in the back seat.

"That thought occurred to me, too," she said. "But I think the explanation is simpler than that. They're a Republican power couple, living inside their right-wing bubble. They sincerely thought nobody would freak out. They thought it was a good idea. Boswell is prouder than hell of his pro-fracking stance, despite the ambivalence of his position paper. For him to pressure Regional Oil to box up those drill bits doesn't make any sense."

"Republican women creep me out," Jennifer said.

"Me too but don't say that in public," I warned her. "We need a whole lot of them to cross over if we're going to win this campaign."

"Seriously, though," Jennifer continued, "what kind of woman thinks it's a good idea to slap a coat of pink paint on the big mechanical dick she intends to use to rape the actual earth?"

"The corporate executive kind, that's what," Dan said.

"The more I think about it," July said, "I don't think this is about Mrs. Boswell keeping secrets. And, I also think it's more than just a lousy decision on their part.

It's all so weird. It's as though they're trying to keep the spotlight off of something else."

"Let's keep digging," I said. "See if we can find what they're trying to hide."

We pulled up to the hospital's loading dock. Jennifer's job was to go inside and find the public relations director who would meet us at the service door off the cafeteria. To me, this covert behavior seemed like overkill, yet Dan and July insisted and Jennifer wasn't arguing with them for once. To keep the peace, I went along. I even wore sunglasses.

Why is sneaking in a back door considered inconspicuous? Why weren't we as concerned with the hospital orderlies and sanitation teams and food service workers seeing my face as we were with the general public upstairs? Why did we think these people were any less likely to recognize me? If they did, why did their gaze on me matter less?

As we traipsed awkwardly through the service corridor, all these black and brown faces glanced up, took in the scene, and then turned away from us as we passed, directing their attention back to the jobs that made the hospital run.

I thought about the invisibility of working people. This is my job, I reminded myself. To make them visible. To compel us to see—to really understand—the work it takes and the price others pay for our comfort and for our health. The price we all pay for corporate profit.

The guys on my brother's rig, breathing in the benzene so we have gas to heat our homes and cook our food. The women spending long hours bending over the machines in the hospital laundry, ruining their backs and wrecking their feet so our bed sheets are crisp and clean when we fall ill or when we give birth or when it's time to die.

It's working people who meet these basic needs, who make possible our fundamental human comforts. And, it's working people who are pushed aside when the company or the country finds them unprofitable.

Thoughts like these fire me up and turn me inside out. They always have ever since I was a child.

By the time we got to the chemo room, I was operating in a haze of irritation and indignation, compounded by the fear of chemotherapy. I'd been scheduled for a round of ten treatments. This would be my seventh. I'd been horrified to discover that chemo gets harder not easier with each successive treatment.

For the first week after a round of chemo I would feel like shit, naturally, and then just as I was feeling human again, it was time to go back for another dose of chemicals. Since chemo began, I'd been living through a cycle of spending the bad days and even the good days before my next treatment, distracted by dread and feeling sorry for myself for not having a spouse to feel sorry for me.

I would remember the cruel sharpness of the nausea, the twitching limbs, the distended abdomen, the debilitating fatigue. Yet, as bad as the symptoms were, I knew next time would be worse - and the time after that, worse still. Until, like Election Day, the ordeal would suddenly be over and relief would come.

As the nurse swabbed my chemo port with alcohol and prepared the saline drip, Jennifer settled into a visitor's chair, plugged a pair of earbuds into her head, and turned on her iPad. Jennifer's other job duty was to sit here with me as they first pumped me with Benadryl and steroids to prepare my body, then to hang around for about an hour after they filled my veins with the chemo toxins. That first hour of treatment was rather pleasant. Of course that was well before the wave of heat that would rise to my cheeks, as if someone had stoked the furnace, and my face would go red and the queasiness would begin. The chair was comfortable, the headphones noise-cancelling, the privacy curtain pulled around my recliner.

I turned up the volume on the Dixie Chicks to drown out the noises of discomfort from the other chemo patients beyond the curtain. I responded to emails, Jennifer nudging me every once in a while to read aloud to me some news tidbit from her Twitter feed.

The second hour of chemotherapy was always different. To spare my niece the ugliness to come, her witnessing the pain and sweating and vomiting and my creative profanity, her mother would arrive to take her place. When I was in that kind of vulnerable pain, Tina was the only person I wanted around me anyway.

She'd been there from the beginning, when I woke up from the surgery where they'd taken off my areola and all the milk glands. And now she was there for the chemo. Tina had become my sounding board, my collaborator, my wig consultant. She nosed her way into every detail of my treatment and made her opinion known on every decision I faced. She appointed herself my healthcare consultant and wielded her power over the campaign staff with an unbending ferocity.

Certainly she and Jennifer were in cahoots. The girl was continually texting her mother to report what I'd eaten and how long I'd napped. As intrusive as they were, though, I was grateful. It's hard to be sick when you're single and harder yet when you're in the public eye.

Soon the guy from the pharmacy would arrive with the bright green Ziploc bag containing my custom-ordered chemo cocktail. My stomach churned at the thought of that bag. We were nearing Election Day and lurking on my calendar between then and now were more chemo sessions. The nasty side effects of both the treatment and the campaign would only keep getting more intense. I lay my head back against the pillow, closed my eyes, and tried to think about something else. Maybe sleep would come. It didn't, but soon enough Tina showed up, taking my mind off the terrible anticipation of the chemo bag.

Jennifer kissed us both and left, dashing to campus for her political science class. Tina sat at my side, exhaled, and began telling me about our father's latest escapade. Since he retired from Regional Oil, he'd found purpose in life by starting a Neighborhood Watch program, a project that interested exactly nobody but himself. He stopped organizing meetings due to chronic low attendance and now just patrolled the streets alone. Every night he put on a McGruff the Crime Dog T-shirt and walked the already low-crime subdivision where he and my mother have lived for thirty years. Giving him crap about his hobby became a family pastime.

"He found the dog that's been tearing up the Anderson's garden," Tina told me. "Mom says he came home covered in mud and dog slobber, dragging this adorable mutt into the kitchen—"

My privacy curtain parted and a nurse entered, carrying that goddamn bright green bag. "Shit," I said.

"Nice to see you, too, Councilmember," she said brightly.

"Sorry," I said.

"Oh, no worries. I get that a lot," she said. She hung the bag on the pole and detached my saline drip. She caught the swinging end of the chemo tube and glanced up at the bag before she attached it to the port in my arm.

"Huh," she said, withdrawing the tube. "That's odd. Your name isn't William."

"Nope," I said.

"And your last name? It's spelled G-L-A-S-S, right?"

I nodded, even as she blushed. Everyone in Greenville knew my name.

Another nurse carrying a bright green chemo bag drew back the curtain. Wordlessly, the two nurses looked at one another. They double-checked the names on their bags.

"I've got Margaret," the new nurse said.

"I've got William," said the nurse at my side.

"Switcheroo," said the new nurse.

"Yup," said the other.

Tina had a very odd look on her face, like she'd eaten something spoiled.

"Wait," I said. "William Glass?"

A male voice came from the other side of my privacy curtain. "Oh for fuck sake," it said.

"Billy?" I said, grabbing the curtain to my left and jerking it aside.

There was my brother, hooked up to a saline drip.

My sister began to laugh. "Oh my god," she said. "This is just too perfect." She stood beside my chair doubled over in spasms, guffawing.

Billy was getting chemo.

He smiled at me. Raised his eyebrows and screwed up his mouth in an expression of irony. "Hey, kiddo," he said.

"Billy?" I said, my mind reeling and my stomach in nauseous knots. "Cancer?"

"Serves you both right," Tina spat, unable to regain her composure.

"I've been hiding behind this curtain," he confessed. "I heard you come in and I couldn't escape." He took in the scene. Me hooked up to a chemo bag. "Jesus Christ, Sis."

He turned to Tina. "You knew about Peg?"

Dumbly, I repeated. "You knew about Billy?"

"You both made me swear not to tell," she said, wiping her eyes. "You're each a couple of dipshits, you know that? I can't tell you how lucky I feel to be here to witness this moment."

"Shut up a minute, Tina," Billy said.

"Well, you're getting what you deserve," Tina said.

We each turned our incredulous faces toward our big sister.

"Oh, no," she said. "Oh no, I didn't mean that. Damn. You guys…" She inhaled as if to laugh again but instead a deep sob emerged. "Oh, you guys," she said, reaching again for the box of Kleenex, now crying as hard as she'd been laughing.

"What kind you got, Peg?" Billy asked me. "What kind? You got it bad?"

"Breast," I said. "It's not so bad. I had the surgery. They cut away a pretty good chunk. I'm halfway through the chemo. They're saying it looks good. Like they probably got it all."

Finally, I met his eye. I was so afraid to ask. I knew what it would be. I've known for years. When a family has three generations of men working at Regional Oil, the odds of it are pretty certain.

"Leukemia," he said.

"You guys," Tina said. "We're in hell. The whole family. We're insane with worry."

"Wait! Everyone knows?" I said. "Everyone knows I have cancer and Billy has cancer and we haven't told one another?"

"Of course everyone knows," she told me. "Everyone agrees you're being idiots. Somehow we all agreed to go along with it. Nobody wanted to be the one to tell you."

I reached out my hand for Billy's, who reached back and took it. Our fingers entwined in the space between our chemo recliners. "I'm so sorry," I told him.

"We've always been good at lying to one another," he said.

"Shut up, you," I said, squeezing his hand.

Chapter Seven

I was summoned to the family homestead by the elders. It was time for a Glass Family Meeting.

When I arrived, my father and Billy were planted on the couch, watching the game. My mother and Tina were in the kitchen, hustling out a three-course dinner for six, like it was no big thing. My grandfather arrived, kissed the women in the kitchen, and went to join the boys in front of the television.

How a feminist like myself arose from this household remains a mystery to everyone. My ex-husband used to say my mother must've gotten knocked up by the UPS delivery man.

Tina and Billy left their spouses and kids at home, certainly at the request of our mother, who has always treated Glass Family Meetings like a sacred rite. When dinner was ready and we all sat at the table—me and my siblings and our grandfather and our parents—it was as though I was sixteen again. Tina was home from college and Grandpa was over for dinner in the middle of the week because Grandma recently died and he wasn't much of a cook.

Tonight Tina would be missing dinner with her husband as well as Jennifer and her two teenage brothers. Billy's wife would be feeding their kids and putting them to bed alone. Me, I left nobody at home but my cat, Fred.

I know Tina loves her life and I'm glad for her, but I know, too, that my mother hated hers. She was too smart, too ambitious, and too curious to be a 1970's housewife. I grew up feeling her sadness and frustration. I resolved in my twenties I would not make the decisions she did. And I haven't. Apart from being childless, another disappointment of my failed marriage, I was glad not to have followed in her footsteps.

My father gracelessly recited the dinner prayer, the same series of words he's intoned since the day he married my mother and took his seat at the head of the dinner table. He said the words as automatically as the Pledge of Allegiance, just a series of sentences to get over with before we can eat.

He waited until we loaded our plates and were cutting into the pot roast. He swallowed a gulp of wine and said he supposed the Glass Family Meeting should go ahead and come to order. "I've asked you all to come here tonight—" he began.

"We've asked you," interrupted my mother. "Your grandfather and your father and me."

"We've asked you here—" he tried again.

"To tell me and Peg we've been acting like a couple of assholes," said Billy. "Message received."

"Yes, indeed," I said. "Pass the salt?"

"Nice try," said Tina.

"Well, that's not quite all—" my mother said.

"Listen," my grandfather said.

"Okay, folks," my father said.

"Great pot roast, Ma," said Billy.

We stopped talking all at once and I took quick advantage of the sudden silence. I slid back my chair and stood. I raised my glass. Little speeches of this sort were not uncommon at Glass Family Meetings.

"Okay, I understand," I said. "I get it. Billy didn't tell me about his diagnosis"-I still couldn't bring myself to say leukemia—"because he knew I'd get on my high horse about the benzene. And he was right. If I were him, I wouldn't have told me either. I'm a terrible sister and a terrible person and I apologize to everyone."

They watched me in silence. I stood there, glass raised, then I inhaled and uttered the family toast that my mother invented two decades ago at the lake house we used to rent every year. That night my father took us kids rowing and lost an oar in the middle of the water and we ended up drifting for three hours and finally walking five miles around the lake to the cabin, to be greeted by a cold dinner and my scared and angry mother. She shouted at my father even as she was kissing his face and weeping in relief. Later, over reheated spaghetti, she stood at the table overcome by the health and safety of her loved ones and coined the toast.

"May you fuck it up grandly," I told them, "and be forgiven in full."

"To fucking it up and to forgiving," recited my family, like a liturgy. We clinked our glasses and drank our wine. I sat down. We all chewed on the pot roast for a few minutes.

"That's out of the way," said my grandfather.

"What? There's more?" Billy said.

My grandfather began cutting his meat with noisy vigor. This of course meant that he had something to say. We all waited as he put a forkful of meat and potatoes in his mouth, chewed purposefully, and swallowed. As a family, we were extraordinarily well-trained.

"Your father and I were thinking," he began.

Tina made a murmuring noise and when I looked up she was raising her eyebrows at her dinner plate as if to say, *okay, here we go.*

"We've given three generations to the company," he said. "Father, son, grandson. We've made a good living."

"We've helped people," my father said. "We've made a difference."

"No sharper roughneck than a Glass man," Billy said, and they all nodded in agreement at the aphorism they'd been sharing over barbeques and campfires since before Billy could speak.

"And this is bullshit," said my grandfather. "This cancer? It's bullshit."

"Bullshit," said my father, nodding at his pot roast.

"Bullshit," echoed my mother, looking me levelly in the eye.

This is not what I expected.

"What are you geezers going on about?" Billy said.

"Two of our children with cancer," my father said. "That's what."

"It's scary as hell," said my grandfather. "It's not right."

"The company should pay," said my mother.

Our forks went still as we all looked at her. "Mom?" Tina said. "Are you serious?" Even more than the men in our family, my mother had always been a diehard supporter of Regional Oil. For two years she was chairwoman of the Roughneck Wives Association, organizing Labor Day picnics and charity drives and welcome baskets for new families. The company kept her family fed, she used to tell us, and she saw it as an extension of her motherly role to support the institution that supplied the paychecks.

She tolerated her husband and son's membership in the labor union but any time there was talk of a strike she'd discourage it with such vigor that I used to wonder why the men bothered to pay union dues at all. With my mother in charge of the domestic sphere, they were accustomed to living without collective bargaining at home, never mind in the workplace.

So, it was bizarre to hear her suggesting Regional Oil should be held accountable for Billy's cancer. She was fond of proclaiming that she didn't believe in the harmful effects of fracking any more than she believed in gay marriage.

"I'm stunned, Mom," I said.

"Oh stop it," she replied. "Do you think I'm some kind of monster? Or a Fox News parrot? I can think for myself. For God's sake, the company needs to stop giving their employees leukemia!"

"Whose family is this?" I said. "Have I landed in a parallel universe?"

"Keep rubbing it in," my mother said quietly. "See where it gets you."

"So what do you expect me to do about it?" Billy said. "There's nothing to be done. I'm lucky to have health insurance."

"You'd be luckier not to have leukemia," said my grandfather, "which, by the way, isn't just a stroke of bad luck. We all know it. Excavating the gas the way we used to do it is one thing. This new process—this fracking—it's bad. It's bad news all around. The company needs to stop."

"They won't, Pop," Billy said. "They've put a hundred million dollars into research and development on fracking technology. They aren't about to stop anytime soon."

"Billy's right," I said. "They won't stop. Not on their own."

"Well, then," my mother said, "someone needs to make them." She gazed at me pointedly, until they were all looking at me. "Last time I checked, someone at this table was an elected representative."

"What?" I said. "I'm trying! I've been trying for years! I vote against Regional Oil every chance I get. You all know this."

"The problem," my father said, "is you're trying the old fashioned way."

"You mean, like, through legislation?" I said. "Democracy?"

"Extreme times call for extreme measures," said my grandfather.

"What are you people cooking up?" Billy said. He was eyeing the three oldsters like he'd just figured something out.

"I think you know, son," said my mother. "We're talking about what happened on the well pad last February."

"What?" I said, searching one face, then the next. "What happened?"

"We've discussed this, Mom," Billy said.

"That was before you got cancer," she replied.

"The accident last February didn't give me leukemia," he told her. "Don't be ridiculous."

"What accident?" I said.

"We didn't want to tell you," my father said.

My grandfather cleared his throat. "But we're telling you now."

"This is about that storage tank?" Tina said. "The one that blew up?"

"For crissake," I said. "Again I'm the last to know anything."

Billy turned back to his dinner, pushing the beef and carrots around his plate. I realized his appetite must have been as lousy as mine. We were both on our third day, post-chemo. I was aching and perspiring and my mother's roast—a dinner I normally can't get enough of—was making me want to puke. I could only imagine Billy's discomfort, given the intensity of his chemo cocktail compared to mine.

"Here's what happened, Sis," he said softly. "A number of months ago, a tank filled with fluid—what exactly it was the company won't say—ruptured and leaked fluid into the ground at the well site."

"Well, that's an understatement," my grandfather said. "The goddamn thing ignited. It flew up like a rocket and landed fifty feet away."

"How large was this storage tank?" I asked.

"About the size of a tractor-trailer," Billy replied. "They were flushing the frack lines. The tank ruptured and somehow ignited."

"A worker was hurt, isn't that right?" Tina said.

"Joey Federico," said my father. "He's paralyzed."

"What the hell?" I said. "Why wasn't this in the news? Why didn't I hear about this?"

"If Joey had died they might have reported on it," my mother said.

"Happens all the time," my grandfather said. "The company's been cited for 21 environmental violations and 38 OSHA violations in the past three years."

"Geez, Pops," Billy said. "You've been doing your research."

"I figured out the internet," he said. "Took a class down at the community center. Those kids running the computer lab are pretty sharp. Not to mention interested in the subject. It turns out that fracking operations all over the place have the same kind of violation records."

"Let's get to the point," my father said.

"There's a point?" I asked him.

"It's time for the family to step up," said my grandfather.

"I guess you're going to tell us how," Billy observed.

"No, actually," my mother said. "We thought we'd leave that part up to you."

"What do you expect me to do about it, Mom?" Billy said. "The company does what it wants. I'm a nobody, I'm just a goddamn roughneck. And thanks to your daughter here, I'm already in trouble with the brass."

"That exploded tank..." my mother said. "And your leukemia."

"There's no way to connect those two events, Mom," he said.

"I know that," she said. "But I've had it. I've just had enough." She reached across the table and laid her palm on my forearm. "Two sick children. I can't bear it. And Peggy, don't try to tell me your rare breast cancer isn't caused by environmental factors. I know how to use the internet, too. I'm done apologizing for the company. Not after what it's done to my children."

"What do you propose, Mom?" said Billy. "Do you want to just firebomb the place? How about we all get dressed in our matching family ninja outfits and break into the plant and sabotage the fracking drills?"

"Now you're making fun of me," she told him.

"Since when have old people needed to tell young people how to make trouble?" my father asked.

"Who are you calling young, Dad?" Tina said. "Your baby boy here is 50 years old."

"With a wife and two kids, let's not forget," Billy said. "If I get fired, our lives go to shit. You think we're screwed now? Wait until I lose my health insurance."

"Tell them, Billy," my father said. "Tell them what you told me."

"I'm no whistleblower, Dad," Billy said. "Don't make me into one."

"Nobody is asking you to call the papers, son."

He screwed up his face in the same frown he's been making at me since we were kids. "Like telling Peg here isn't the same damn thing."

"Hey," I said. "Don't be a jerk. I'm your sister."

"We'll take it a step at a time," my mother said. "We will trust one another."

Billy turned to me. "I was working that day. When the tank blew up. Which meant it was up to me to write up the accident report."

My grandfather interrupted, his fork stabbing the air. "And he was ordered not to write it! Not to put it into the computer!"

"By whom?" I asked.

"My supervisor," Billy said. "Baxter Sherman. He told me to let it drop. He said the orders came from upstairs and that he hadn't asked any questions and neither should I."

"This sounds a lot like what happened with the drill bits," I said.

"No kidding," Billy said.

"It's a cover-up!" my grandfather croaked.

"Okay," said Tina, "so the company didn't report an industrial accident. These things happen every day. What the hell are we supposed to do about it?"

"Yes, well," my mother replied. "It's not every day that two of my children end up with cancer. What are we going to do about it? I have no idea. But nobody's leaving this house until we have a plan."

She put on a pot of coffee and brought out a cherry pie and the Glass Family Meeting carried on until midnight. We stayed at the table until we figured out what we were going to do next.

Chapter Eight

The first thing that shocks me about Mercedes' grandmother is that she's perhaps the smallest woman I've ever seen. She shakes my hand and smiles. Her gaze on me is long and appraising and makes me feel anxious about having added her to my list of visitors.

The second thing that shocks me is her voice. It is rough, low, and raspy. Mercedes has performed enough impersonations of her grandmother that I shouldn't be surprised but, nonetheless, the incongruity is jarring. The old lady has apparently never had a cigarette in her life, yet she wound up sounding like a chain-smoker anyway.

She settles herself next to Mercedes onto one of those seats that are bolted to the floor. She holds her purse in her lap. The tips of her toes just touch the linoleum. Her shoes are sensible and shined and she wears wool hose. The three of us sit there in silence for a few seconds, too long for comfort.

"Mercedes has told me so much about you," she says politely.

"Why your English is perfect!" I say, before I can stop myself. Then I freeze. Surely she'll take offense. What a stupid, racist thing to say.

She gives me a hard, unsmiling look.

"Forgive me, Mrs. Quinto, I say.

"Abuelita is an English teacher," Mercedes says.

"A tutor, mi'ja, not a teacher," the old lady corrects. She turns to me. "Only to the kids in the neighborhood sometimes. After school I help them with their homework." Her accent is distinct yet hard to place. Her pronunciation is careful, correct, and flavored richly by Central America.

"Mercedes tells me at your job they think you don't speak any English at all."

"Oh, surely, they think I'm illiterate," Mrs. Quinto says. "They probably think I speak one of those ignorant *Indio* jungle languages that you can't even write down."

Aha, so I'm not the only reflexive racist here. "But you're fluent in two tongues," I say, trying too hard. "I'm so impressed."

"She speaks Portuguese, too," Mercedes says.

"Not really," her grandmother replies.

"Last year you read that whole book in Portuguese!" Mercedes says.

"My mother was Brazilian," Mrs. Quinto tells me. "My father was American. I grew up in Mexico City, then we moved to Texas when I was a teenager."

"And she came to Greenville after she and my grandfather got married," Mercedes says.

I am aware of the tick of the clock on the wall and the guard's looming presence at the door. They only give us twenty minutes for visitors. "I'm sorry to be so blunt," I say, "but Mercedes tells me you work at Regional Oil? And that sometimes you clean the executives' locker room?"

"Slobs," she says. "Seriously. You just know they got another lady just like me at home, following them around cleaning up their messes."

"Who are they?" I ask. "Do you know their names? Would you recognize their faces if you saw pictures of them?" I was thinking I could get July to bring me a copy of the Regional Oil annual report and we could ask Mrs. Quinto to point out the people she has seen in the locker room.

She shoots a look at her granddaughter. "Esta señora piensa que soy una idiota," she told her.

"Yes," Mercedes says to me. "I think it's safe to say that she knows who they are."

"June Saunders, Senior V.P. of Operations," Mrs. Quinto says, holding out her hand to tick off names on her fingers. "Eleanor Allison, V.P. of Public Relations. Dorothy Charles, CFO. And sometimes Sheila Maguire herself. But usually, that one, she exercises at five o'clock in the morning. Like a crazy skinny lady, all by her lonesome in that great big gym."

As Mrs. Quinto recites the names and titles of the top management at Regional Oil, I am managing to retrieve the word "*piensa*" from some dusty corner of my mind and am realizing that Mrs. Quinto just said that I must think she's an idiot.

"I've offended you again," I say.

"I've forgiven you again," she replies.

"What do they talk about? These ladies?" I ask.

"Their personal bests. They never stop talking about their personal bests. How many miles they ran on the treadmill. How many pounds they lifted above their heads. How many jobs they eliminated in their departments. I want to say to them, 'You want to hear about *my* personal best? Yesterday, I cleaned fifty toilets. But that was nothing compared to my personal best back in 2005, the day a pipe in the basement broke and I mopped up about a hundred gallons of raw sewage in less than two hours. That was my personal best. A hundred buckets full of poop.'"

"Abuelita doesn't like her job very much," Mercedes says.

"Do they talk about business, too?" I ask.

"When they're not talking about personal bests, they're talking about business. It's like these ladies don't have families or hobbies. They don't go to parties. They don't go on dates. However, they do have very flat stomachs and muscular legs. Today they were talking about a charity event, a running thing. They've been taking long lunches to run around in circles on the roof. You should see the matching outfits. Bright pink."

"Not the Race for Cancer Research," I say.

"Yep," Mrs. Quinto says.

Mercedes gasps. She knows the whole story, of course. "Those bitches," she says, nudging my elbow. "Next she'll tell you the pink drill bits are back."

Her grandmother squints at Mercedes in suspicion. "How do you know about the pink drill bits?"

"How did *you* know about the pink drill bits, Grandma?" Mercedes replies, a little smile on her face. She's enjoying herself. It strikes me how much she must miss her grandmother. How much she must miss her dead mother.

"They were talking about those drills in the locker room. They had a nasty name for it." She waves her hand dismissively. "A cultural reference I didn't understand. A film, I think. It's not important."

"Grandma, how do you know it was nasty if you didn't understand?"

"I knew," she says. "Those ladies, they talk about sex like they're men."

"Sex? How are we suddenly talking about sex, Grandma?"

"The drill bit," I say.

"Right," Mrs. Quinto says.

Mercedes gasps. "They called it something sexual? The lady executives have a dirty nickname for the pink drill bit? Please, Grandma, you've got to remember. I need to know, I really do."

Mrs. Quinto and I look at Mercedes in silence. Without warning an image of my ex-husband's penis pops into my head. He did have a nice dick, I have to admit.

"What?" Mercedes says. "I'm curious. Also I'm bored. Come on, Grandma."

"It's undignified," her grandmother says, her gravelly voice bringing weight to the opinion. "I won't repeat it."

"It's okay, Grandma. You don't have to say anything, I'll just guess."

"No you won't, young lady," Mrs. Quinto says. She turns to me. "What else can I help you with, Councilmember Glass?"

"You're willing to help?" I say.

"It depends," she says. "What are you trying to do? What do you want?"

I hesitate. I'm not sure how much I should tell her. But if she's going to be of any use, she needs to know the basics. "There was a cover up," I say, "of an industrial accident that happened last February on one of the well pads."

"You mean that storage tank that went flying?" Mrs. Quinto asks.

"Is there anything you don't know?" I say.

"Big Daddy?" Mercedes guesses.

"What?" Mrs. Quinto says.

"The nasty nickname," she says. "Is that it? Is that what the ladies called it?"

"Don't be disgusting. No."

"The accident," I say, "the storage tanks. How did you know?"

"Everybody knows," says Mrs. Quinto. "Afterward there weren't the normal procedures. The inspectors never came. When these things happen, the inspectors are supposed to come and talk to everybody—even to the janitorial staff. Especially the janitorial staff. For some reason, they think people like me are spending our time at work dumping barrels of hazardous waste into the river. So, they come to the plant and they sit in a room all day long and ask everybody the same questions. It's the same routine every time. Every time some little safety problem happens. But this time, when it's a big safety problem—a whole tank, blowing sky high—nothing. Nobody comes to investigate. That poor man is in a wheelchair now. He won't ever walk again."

"I was trying to get proof that they hid the accident," I tell her. "That's what landed me in jail."

"What kind of proof?"

"Memos, emails, etcetera."

"Porky the Pig?" Mercedes says.

"No," her grandmother says. "Stop."

She turns to me. "If you wanted proof of the accident, all you had to do was talk to the employees."

I set aside this bit of wisdom to contemplate later. How ironic if she were right. What if all along there were more employees like Billy and Mrs. Quinto at Regional Oil, people willing to risk their jobs? What if all we needed to do was ask them to speak up? What if I never needed to break the law at all?

"You haven't answered my question," Mrs. Quinto says. "What do you want?"

"I want to expose their cover up. I think that fuel tank accident represents something else. I think it was a symptom. It happened for a reason and they know what that reason is. They need to keep it hidden because it's something very big."

"And you want me to overhear all this?"

She has a point. It is unlikely the ladies would rehash the whole debacle in the locker room. And even if they did, testimony from the cleaning woman hardly constitutes a strong case. "Actually we'd need documents. Correspondence," I say.

Mrs. Quinto studies my face. Her expression is unreadable. I plow on. "Do you have access to other parts of the building?" I ask.

"She doesn't need access to anywhere else," Mercedes says. "Everything you need is in the locker room."

"What are you talking about?" I say.

"Their cell phones. They leave them in their lockers when they go running, right?"

"No," I say. "I'm guessing they wouldn't. They probably make calls while they're on the track. Listen to music."

"In the shower, though," Mercedes says.

"Yes," I say, "in the shower."

Now it's Mercedes and me doing the scheming. She's a half-a-step ahead of me. "She couldn't steal their phones. They'd notice right away."

"And accuse the cleaning lady first," I say.

"She'd need to access the data somehow," Mercedes says.

"Download their email inboxes," I whisper, thinking aloud. "Can she do that in a few minutes? Is that even possible?"

"Five minutes," shouts the guard from the other side of the room.

"Damn," I say.

Mrs. Quinto reaches for her sweater. Suddenly my mind is flooded with dirty jokes about fracking machinery. "Wait," I say. "When did you hear the executives talking about the pink drill bits? Back in September, right?"

"No," Mrs. Quinto says. "This was last Thursday."

I smack my forehead in disbelief. We'd seen this coming. Regional Oil had never really scrapped the drill bit campaign. They just put the bits in storage, waiting until after the election. Now that the election is over and I'm in jail, the Regional Oil executives are free to display their lady bits for everyone to see. Just in time for the Race for Research.

"The Pink Peter," I say. "That's their secret nickname, isn't it?"

"Si," says Mrs. Quinto "you guessed it."

"You've got to admit it's pretty funny," Mercedes says.

"Will you help us, Mrs. Quinto?" I ask.

She hooks her purse over her shoulder. "Let me get this straight. You want me to wait until the ladies are in the shower, go into their lockers, turn on their phones, and steal their emails?"

"Grandma, these people are making everybody sick," Mercedes says. "They're ruining the earth. They don't care if their employees are hurt. Or even killed."

Mrs. Quinto stands up. We all stand up. She pulls her granddaughter into a hug. She strokes her face lovingly and gives her a sad smile. "Mi'ja," she coos.

Then she turns to me. "Maybe I came here today because I believed you were innocent or maybe just because I wanted to see for myself that you're an honest person."

"Thank you," I say. "Now you see, right?"

"I see, yes," she replies. "I see why you're here in this jailhouse, Councilmember. You're here for asking another person to steal for you, right?"

"Grandma," Mercedes says. Tears have sprung into her eyes. "Don't be rude. Please. She's just trying—"

"En nuestra familia no somos ladrones," the old lady says.

"But that's not true, Abuela. I *am* a thief," Mercedes tells her. "I stole, remember?"

"Not any more, sweetheart," Mrs. Quinto says. She reaches into her purse for a Kleenex and wipes her granddaughter's cheeks. "You've put that behind you. That's the difference between you and your friend here. She's looking for a chance to learn twice from the same mistake."

Mrs. Quinto reaches for my hand, shakes it firmly, and is gone.

Chapter Nine

F ive weeks before Election Day and I was spending my Saturday as I've spent at least a hundred others: walking the neighborhoods of Greenville. As a three-term incumbent I know a few things about knocking on doors.

If it were earlier in the campaign, I would have invited a big donor or an influential fundraiser to walk alongside me for the day. But because there were so few weeks to go, I needed every minute I could get with my staff. So July and I were planning to canvass together and do some campaign business as we walked.

July had been doing a reasonably decent job as my campaign manager. Before she worked for me, she managed the campaign of a state representative I knew, a guy who won the seat handily, even though he seemed plainly underqualified. She was a serious sort, almost morose, yet she was efficient and reliable and passionate about the work. We were close to the election, the period when staffers become obsessed with their roles beyond the campaign. July hadn't yet approached me about serving on my permanent staff, but I knew she would.

At Democratic headquarters, we did the usual volunteer meet-and-greet with doughy bagels and warmish coffee. I gave a speech that felt routine but seemed to adequately rouse the troops. There were about thirty walkers that morning, a pretty decent turnout. A half dozen of them were from Frack Free Greenville, the exceedingly well-organized activist group that was part of a national coalition of grass-roots organizations. These people represented a real interest group and constituted a key element of my voter base. They had my back and I had theirs.

Although a few students and a couple of families showed up, the bulk of the day's volunteer force came from the Fan Club. They were nothing if not reliable. And, as surely as their utter lack of interests outside of Democratic Party politics made them lousy dinner guests, it also made them superior canvassers. These people were so well versed in current events and the liberal versus conservative perspective on every issue, it was as though they slept at night in a marinade of MSNBC, The Huffington Post, and The Daily Show.

July grabbed our walk list and we got in our cars. We left mine at the end of the route and parked hers at the beginning. We began our canvass with a whole lot to talk about and a whole lot of houses to cover.

Nobody was home at the first three addresses, so we whizzed through several items on July's agenda. The approval of our next robo-call script; my upcoming meeting with the *Star's* editorial board to lobby for their endorsement, which as far as we could tell was mine to lose; and the campaign finance report due to the Elections Board the following day.

"Next," she said. "Regional Oil. You said we should do some digging."

"Right. We need to know why they scrapped the pink drill bit campaign with such..." I searched for the word.

"Alacrity," said July, opening a chain link gate to the front yard of the next house on our list.

"Right. Alacrity."

She rang the doorbell. Inside a little dog started barking. "First, I think we should assume they haven't ditched the Boland sponsorship entirely," July said as we waited for someone to come to the door. "My guess is that they're just setting it aside until after the election. Those drill bits are probably in a warehouse somewhere, waiting for November."

"Makes sense," I said. Through the tinted glass on the front door I could see a shadow moving around inside the house. Something about the place seemed familiar. Like I'd been here before. In a town the size of Greenville, you end up in a lot of peoples' homes. "It also adds up that they didn't see the obvious, that the drill bits were political poison," I told her. "I'm certain they got a call from the Boswell campaign."

"Just what Dan and I suspected." She frowned at the door and rang the bell again. "So we started thinking about people who might have insight into the nature of the current relationship between Boswell and Regional Oil."

"It's damn cozy, we already know that."

"Yes," she said. "But how cozy exactly? I called your former consultant Manuel in DC and he said he'd sniff around a bit. And guess what he found out."

The front door opened. A young woman in a bathrobe stood there, looking at us. She had clearly just come from bed. We had woken her up. I recognized her immediately as my ex-husband's cousin, Rita.

"What," she said.

She didn't seem to recognize me. I held my breath anyway and didn't say a word. I recalled the hideous green dress she wore to my wedding.

July apologized for disturbing her. Rita informed us she works nights and we were interrupting her REM sleep, bigtime, so we should tell her what we want. As if sleepwalking—which in fact maybe she was, who knows—she listened without expression to July's canned pitch, took our campaign literature, said thank you. This is typical of my interaction with constituents. Either it's the guy who wants to argue with you or the woman who wants you to just go away or it's someone from your past that you really don't want to talk to. I really didn't want to talk to Rita.

Finally, she looked at the campaign brochure in her hand, then up at me.

"Peg," she said. "Is that you?"

"Rita?" I said, feigning surprise. "Wow."

"It has been a few years," she said.

"Almost seven, I think," I said.

We stood there smiling politely.

"How's your mom?" Rita said.

"Happy," I told her. "Always with her projects, you know."

Here is where I was supposed to ask about my ex. The one who cheated on me, and who asked his cousin Rita to cover for him, which she did, because the woman he was fucking was Rita's best friend. In fact, now that I stood there thinking about it, I remembered why this house was familiar. This was the front porch I stood on, banging on the door like a fool and shouting accusations at my husband. This is the house where he used to bring his girlfriend.

"Get out the vote, huh?" Rita said.

"Good to see you, Rita," I said, and took July by the elbow. We turned and walked back through her front yard.

"What was that all about?" July said.

"Old business," I told her. We turned down the sidewalk, to the next address.

"So," I said, "back to the point. What did Manuel find out?"

"McCray is talking retirement," she said.

Harry McCray was our Senator, a moderate Republican. He was a reasonable guy, if predictably pro-market and unwilling to consider bipartisan anything. He always voted down party lines but on the other hand he wasn't the kind of conservative to lead crusades. He'd been in the seat nearly thirty years. I wasn't surprised to hear he was ready to leave. The Senate was a grueling gig and McCray had stuck it out a long time.

"What was he doing campaigning if he's planning to retire?" I said.

"Repubs are looking to keep a lock on the seat," July said. "McCray is a much easier re-elect than some new guy. Word is he cut a deal with the RNC that he'd run the campaign and then step down early next year. For health reasons. Then the RNC will fill his seat by appointment.

"Who's their heir apparent?" I asked.

"Who do you suppose?" July said. "Boswell."

"Motherfucker," I said. "So my council seat is just his parking space until the Senate job opens up."

She nodded. "But it's important for Boswell to win. They'll have a harder time appointing him if he's never been elected."

"Where'd you hear all this?" I asked.

"Manuel, like I said."

"Where did he get it?"

"I didn't ask. And neither should you. Manuel has his ways."

Regional Oil had always been a major contributor to McCray's campaigns. Our state's campaign finance laws allow PACs to keep their donors secret. But it was commonly presumed our friendly local fracking executives were also heavy backers of an independent McCray PAC or two. If Manuel was right, Regional Oil had found their next Congressional puppet.

Boswell was being groomed by both the company and by the Senator. And he was trying to plow through my council seat to get there.

In the light of the fuel tank explosion cover-up and the company's long-term plans to deepen their influence in Congress, their sudden yanking of the pink drill bit sponsorship was beginning to make sense. Here in the final weeks of the campaign, the company wasn't about to take any chances that they'd draw the wrong kind of attention.

I wanted to tell July about the Glass Family Meeting. The family, however, didn't want anyone—including members of my campaign staff—to know what we were up to. I understood my family's need for secrecy but covert agendas made me nervous. Also, it was inefficient, to say the least, to pay smart people to do their jobs and yet to keep them in the dark.

Still, my mother was right when she said it was unfair to ask my staff to take the risks we were talking about. She was also right when she said they should be kept ignorant for their own protection.

At the next house, an elderly gentleman kept us standing at the door for a full four minutes as he searched for the key to open the security gate. I considered pointing out the fire hazard situation he was living with but thought better of it. Once he got the door open, he planted himself in the doorway and began a detailed lecture on what he called "moral economics." There was a part of me that was ready to invite myself inside, take off my shoes, sit on his couch and listen to the old man talk about the things that stirred his soul. There was another part of me that wanted to walk away from this whole get-out-the-vote charade and go find a bar that served martinis on a Saturday morning.

The old man stopped talking for a minute and July jumped in to remind him to vote. He took the materials and examined the bullet points. His head jerked up. "Fracking!" he said. "Fracking! Don't get me started about fracking!"

I braced myself. You never know which way a conversation like this will go. I've had some of the best and some of the worst encounters of my life standing on the front porches of voters.

"My little great-grandson!" the man shouted. "The baby! Two years old last September! They were living here. My granddaughter, she didn't have a place to go. Her deadbeat boyfriend took off, and so she came to live with me. It was so nice! We took care of one another. I watched the baby while she ran to the store. She cooked dinner sometimes. We were a family, a little family."

The man reached for the doorframe to steady himself. He seemed suddenly unable to speak.

"Sir?" July said.

"He started having nosebleeds," the old man said. "Nosebleeds, I told my granddaughter, no big deal. So what? Right? Kids get nosebleeds. But my granddaughter, she's worried. Mothers! They worry. And a good thing! The boy—he's two! Two years old! He gets a rash. Then he gets diarrhea. Then he starts getting muscle spasms. And we can smell the natural gas, smell the chemicals, all around the house. She takes him in for blood tests. And what do they find?"

"I'm so sorry," I told him.

"Don't be sorry!" he said. "Be listening."

"What did they find, sir?" July said.

"Twelve chemicals. Fracking chemicals. Traces of those chemicals in my great grandbaby's bloodstream. Lead! Mercury! Formaldehyde!"

This guy reminded me of my grandfather. In fact, he probably knew my grandfather. So she took the baby away, he told us. She had to leave. She moved to California. Now he was alone again.

We told him how sorry we were. We assured him I'd be working my hardest to fight the company; that I had been doing so ever since I was elected, and that we needed him and others to speak out. I gave him the warmest version of my politician-self, the best I could do, knowing we could only spend a few minutes with him or we'd never make it through our route. He shook our hands but his energy had drained. We left him leaning against the doorframe, looking out at his overgrown yard.

When we were out of sight, July touched my arm and we stopped on the sidewalk. "Listen," she said. "I'd like to talk about stepping in as your chief of staff. That old man just decided it for me. This shit makes me mad. I want to do something about it."

Last night at my parents' dinner table, we came to the shared conclusion that the fuel tank explosion at Regional Oil was an important event and the company's silencing its employees on the matter was significant. The family identified its mission as gathering intelligence on the accident and its cover-up. What we would do with that information was a question to be answered later, if and when we were lucky enough to succeed in some way.

Even if I couldn't tell July about my family's involvement, there was plenty of other stuff she could know. "Listen," I said, as we headed to the house across the street. I told her about the fuel tank accident and the cover-up. I didn't mention my brother, my father, or my grandfather, but July knew three generations of the Glass family had worked for the company. She certainly saw that I couldn't have gotten this information any other way except from the inside.

"Okay, then,"' she said after she heard the story. "What are we looking for?"

"Evidence," I said. "Emails, memos. From last April."

"That's not the kind of thing that just falls into your lap," she said.

"That's why we need to dig," I told her.

At the next house a woman wearing overalls and work gloves came to the front door. She stepped outside and said hello. She told us she was heading out to feed her chickens and that if we wanted to talk we could join her. We followed her around the side of the house, where she grabbed a feed bucket and headed over to her coop. Inside was a healthy-looking flock of colorful birds.

"What are their breeds?" I asked. "I don't know a thing about chickens."

The woman pointed at a black and white speckled hen. "This is Jenny; she's an Ancona. Those two are Harriet and Lucy; they're Norfolk Greys." She indicated the rest with a sweep of her hand. "The other ladies are all mixed breeds. Good layers."

We watched the chickens scramble for the feed she tossed at them. I welcomed this little break. Canvassing can be interesting work.

"So, Councilmember," said the chicken woman. "What are you doing about Regional Oil?"

"This is the subject on everyone's mind," July said.

"As it should be," she said. "I keep losing chickens."

"What do you mean? They're dying?"

"Two last week. Another one yesterday. And I'm seriously wondering if I should be eating these eggs," she said. She jutted her chin at a goat pen next to the chicken coop. "My nanny gave birth to a deformed kid last month," she said. "No legs."

Then I recognized her. She was one of the protestors who'd been coming to the council meetings every week.

"I want to thank you for your activism," I told her. "We really need people like you in Greenville."

"Too late," she said. She wiped her hands on her overalls. "I'm leaving."

"What do you mean?" July said.

"I'm giving up." She threw her hands in the air halfheartedly. "My house is worthless. I can't sell but I can't stay, either. The air is poison here. The water—" She closed the gate to the henhouse. "Well, it's pointless to keep talking. I've done all the talking I can. I've written letters, I've sat in meetings, I've painted signs, I've damn near screamed myself hoarse at protests. And still they keep dumping poison into the ground, and still it keeps coming back up, and still you politicians keep letting them get away with it."

July jumped in defensively. "The councilmember's record on fracking is one hundred percent in opposition. Her votes have been—"

"Yeah, whatever," she said. "I've heard it all before. I don't mean to be rude, Councilmember, I really don't. But somebody has got to stop this. And we keep electing you and yet it keeps getting worse."

"I'm doing my best," I said lamely.

"I know you are," she replied. "Honestly, I probably couldn't do any better myself. I can't imagine how impossible it must be. How hopeless you must feel some days." She regarded her chickens and her sad goat. "But whatever," she finally said, "it makes no difference to me anymore. I'm moving to Montana next week."

We said our resigned goodbyes and made our way out of her yard. July placed her hand on the latch to the next garden gate but didn't push it open. "What?" I said, looking up from the clipboard.

"I know a guy," July said.

The sun was finally starting to come out from behind the clouds. "A guy?" I said.

"His name is Frankie Brown. He finds emails and memos," she replied.

"Finds them?" I asked. "Where?"

"Frankie is a hacker, Peg. He finds them wherever they are."

Chapter Ten

I'm allowed one visitor per day. Yesterday was Mrs. Quinto. Another day it's my mother. Then it'll be my sister. Tuesday is my trip to Greenville General for my last chemo treatment. Millions of people are in jail in America and so many of them never get visitors, never get to go anywhere, while here I sit with a full social calendar.

My lawyer, however, is allowed unlimited access to me. Today she arrives in a bluster, landing ungracefully in the bolted-down plastic chair, her hair a frizzy mess and her forehead sweating. "We have a lot to cover so let's get busy," she says.

"Hi, Ophelia," I say.

She looks up from her phone. "Sorry. Hi. How's jail?"

Ophelia is an old friend. We went to college together, sharing a suite in the dorm with two other girls. After school, I spent the next twenty years pursuing politics and she set her sights on the law and then on teaching it. She doesn't practice much these days. She just made the tenured faculty in the law school at Greenville State University. Luckily for me, she teaches criminal law. Even luckier, she took my case.

"Cozy," I told her. "How's life on the outside?"

"Cold," she said. "In more ways than one."

She pulled a file from her briefcase. "Yesterday we deposed Frankie Brown," she said.

Frankie Brown was July's incompetent hacker. The one whose mistakes landed me in jail. "What does he have to say for himself?" I asked.

"He worked out a deal with them," she told me. "He's testifying against you."

"That little shit," I said.

"He says he was only your IT guy. Just a campaign volunteer who knew about computers and came around every once in a while to keep things running."

"Can't we prove he did the actual hacking?" I asked. "Passwords or keystroke analysis or cookies or whatever?"

Ophelia smirked. "Cookies?"

"You know what I mean," I said.

"He used the campaign's computer," she said. "He was competent in one thing, which was covering his own ass. It's your word against his."

"So, what's the strategy, Ophelia?" I asked. "What now?"

"We cast his testimony into doubt. We attack his credibility. And July's."

"I thought you said it was all about how much I knew and when I knew it."

The truth is that I knew everything. From the moment at the chicken lady's front gate, when July said she knew a hacker, to the moment days later when the three of us stood over a computer monitor reading those beautifully damning emails, I knew everything. I was up to my neck in it. What had I been thinking?

"That was before Frankie started cooperating and before July was called as a witness. Unless they perjure themselves, they'll testify you were in the room. Our best bet is to cast suspicion on their credibility."

I can't go to prison. Not that I don't deserve it. I know I broke the law. It's just that I'm the only one who can stop Regional Oil and I can't do it from behind bars. I know I sound like a classic, hubristic politician. Still, it's true. My position—disgraced though I may appear to be—gives me a bullhorn. Also, by exposing the company, I will save my reputation, eventually reclaim my council seat, and shut down fracking in this part of the world.

"What about July?" I ask Ophelia. "If I'm found innocent what happens to her?"

"If she's smart, she'll cut a deal right now," Ophelia said. "Cooperate, like Frankie. None of this will be good for her career."

"There's an understatement," I said. As things stand now, July's career is over. Mine will be, too, unless I expose Regional Oil. The voters love a comeback story. But I need to get back into office before I can do any good.

My brother is dying of cancer. I don't give a damn what anyone says. I'm going to take down the company that is killing him. Let them call me obsessed, it doesn't matter. Maybe I am. If this experience has taught me anything it's that my new job in life is to destroy Regional Oil. They are destroying Greenville and they are destroying the earth and they are destroying my family. For that, they deserve to be shut down. And I deserve to be the person to do it.

"July must absolutely not come back to see you again," Ophelia says. "That was really stupid of her. Of you both. If she comes back, you must refuse to see her."

"How do you know about that?" I say.

"Your mother told me."

"That's the last time I tell her anything," I reply.

"Seriously, July's visit was unwise. It's not about violating the terms of your release anymore; it's that she's a witness for the prosecution. They're not interested in busting her...it's you they want."

"My mother always did like you," I said.

Ophelia sighed. I wasn't giving her the response she wanted. "And I always did like your mother, too."

My mother is especially traumatized to see me behind bars. Politicians normally don't await trial in jail. We're generally not considered high flight risks. Bail is set and posted, and we await our day in court from the comfort of our homes. Unless you're like me, of course, and you violate the terms of your release.

"Why did July come to see you?" Ophelia asks.

"To tell me about the Fan Club," I say.

She looks at me impatiently. Ophelia doesn't like obfuscation.

"They're my die hard supporters," I explain. "They're planning a group run in my honor at the Boland Race for Research."

Ophelia considers this. "That's probably a good thing," she says.

"That's what July said."

"She came here to tell you that?" Ophelia asks. "That's a little odd."

"There's more. She also says the old campaign team has been meeting. At her house. Ostensibly scheming to clear my name."

"That's the silliest thing I've ever heard," Ophelia says. "Everybody's been watching too many legal dramas. What makes your campaign staff think they can clear your name?"

"She didn't go into a lot of detail," I admitted. Could July have been lying? Was it even true that my staff had come back together? Was it true they were still that loyal? What did they hope to accomplish?

"Who's going to these alleged meetings?" Ophelia asks.

"She didn't really say." I feel suddenly like a fool.

"Right. Well. As I said. Next time don't see her. She's not your friend, Peg." She begins gathering her things to leave. She stops shuffling papers and looks hard into my eyes. "How's the cancer?"

"It's okay. My last chemo treatment is next week."

"I'm so sorry I couldn't get you out of here. Your pretrial judge is a masochist."

My judge had been in the same fraternity with Boswell back in college. A conservative ballbreaker. He ignored the screaming newspapers, which for an entire news cycle took a break from their attacks on my character to accuse the judge of kicking me while I was down: DISGRACED AND UNDERGOING CHEMO, POLITICIAN ORDERED BEHIND BARS.

Ophelia had been ticked off to the point of incoherency. The judge denied her request for house arrest, where I would have had an in-home nurse administer the chemo. He approved only a guarded visit to Greenville General and denied an overnight stay in the hospital to recover. The man was taking real pleasure from my pain, a situation I could only rely on karma to rectify. Until then, I would have to endure my worst post-chemo week, tossing and turning on a thin plastic-coated institutional mattress or on my knees on the concrete floor of my cell, puking into a stainless steel toilet.

"It's inhumane," said Ophelia. "That judge should rot in hell."

"Well, at least I've got the sympathy vote."

I am struck for the first time in my life that, given there are 2.5 million incarcerated people in America, statistically that made tens of thousands of people with cancer behind bars. What a lousy way to have the disease. When did we become such an uncaring country?

"At least I have Mercedes," I murmur.

The guard yells that our time is up and Ophelia stands. "Who's Mercedes?" she asks.

"My cellmate. She's a good kid."

Ophelia hugs me and turns to go. She walks three paces away and then comes back. "On second thought, if July shows up here again, you should see her."

"Won't I be held in contempt, too, for violating the terms of my release?"

"Well, you aren't exactly released, are you? It's not like you're initiating anything. If she comes, just listen. See what she has to say. Can't hurt."

I'd almost been ready to trust that woman again. "She must think I'm a complete idiot," I say.

"Be friendly to her," Ophelia advises. "Don't say much, but if she wants to talk, let her. Find out where she stands. It's a huge risk, her coming to see you. She could be held in contempt—

"—and her career wrecked," I finish. But isn't her career already over? Maybe July hadn't been lying last time. Maybe she is indeed out to vindicate me, in part to save herself. It would make sense. Like me, she too believes that exposing Regional Oil will give her career a boost big enough to overcome a felony conviction.

"When's your chemo treatment?" asks Ophelia.

I tell her it's scheduled for next Tuesday. A wave of nausea washes through me at the thought. As promised, the treatments had become increasingly nasty; I am already bracing for the dial being turned up to ten.

"Be tough," she tells me. "There's less than two weeks until trial and then you're going home."

"You're so sure," I say.

"Try not to worry."

Chapter Eleven

After our depressing neighborhood canvass, I found myself in July's living room, watching some redheaded kid named Frankie frown at the screen of the laptop July had stuck in her briefcase on our way out of the office. I grilled her pretty well about Frankie. She told me she's known him for years, since he was in elementary school. She'd been his babysitter during her senior year in high school. Frankie was twelve when she started going over there, too old for a babysitter, really. But he had two little sisters. July babysat for his family throughout college. "He's a good kid," she said. "Complete genius."

"Can he keep a secret?" I asked.

She assured me that Frankie was the kind of person who likes to help. He likes to please. "And yeah," she said, "I've known him to keep a secret or two."

Now I sat next to Frankie on July's couch, watching him work. He frowned at the screen, muttering creative obscenities at the keyboard. I'd never seen anyone type as fast as this kid. He was a bit of an oddball. He wouldn't make eye contact with me. In fact, he hardly looked at me. He was talking only to July, who interpreted the comments I didn't understand. The kid spoke in some kind of tech dialect evidently comprehensible only to skinny geeks who spend their lives in front of computers.

Not understanding a single thing I was seeing on the screen—whatever internet he was using was very different than the one I knew—I got up and stretched my legs. I looked out the window for a while. Checked my email on my phone, replied to some texts. Frankie's fingers tapped the keyboard in the silent room. July stood behind him, looking over his shoulder. She asked a question and appeared to understand his answer. She rested her hand on his shoulder as he worked.

Just as I was about to ask how much longer this thing was going to take, Frankie gasped and said, "Oh my god, we're in."

"Really?" July said.

"I wasn't optimistic there for a minute," Frankie admitted.

"Is he right?" I asked.

"Looks like it," Frankie said. "So we're looking for email correspondence?"

July gave him the date of the fuel tank explosion and a list of keywords and in ninety seconds we were standing over his shoulder reading correspondence that proved a corporate cover up: memos to Sheila Maguire from her management team.

"The well started leaking fracking fluid and spewing oil on Thursday around 08:45," July read from an email written by a crew chief named J. C. Vanderpelt to his supervisor, my brother Billy. The email was forwarded up the chain of command until it reached Maguire's inbox twelve minutes later. "It'll take a couple more days to clear up," July read, still reading Vanderpelt's report. "The well lost control after the blowout preventer failed. It's leaking 50 to 70 barrels per day. We're trucking the fluids away from the site. We're diverting and sandbagging as best we can. . ."

Again, I wondered what the hell I thought I was doing. Hacking into the correspondence of an oil corporation. Not only was it stunningly illegal but the information I was gathering would need to be verified independently or it was worthless.

For a moment, listening to July read aloud one damning email after another, I panicked. I'd gone too far. My brother was right: I was obsessed and I'd lost perspective. But then again, Billy was in the thick of this, too, as was my mother, suddenly the most radical Glass Family activist! Maybe we were all a bit obsessed. Yet who can imagine having two children with cancer? Who can blame her for being a little obsessed?

I thought about the old guy whose young family moved to California. I thought of the woman with the deformed chickens. I'd been playing by the rules for three terms, whacking my head against the cement wall of the fracking industry, losing vote after vote, and someone had to take a stand even if it meant bending the rules. By this time, I was pacing the room, listening to July read the emails aloud.

"Look at this," said July. "An email from Maguire to her senior staff, telling them to file no further reports on the explosion."

I struggled to remember the name of Billy's boss, the one who'd refused to file Billy's report. "Is one of those recipients named something like Sherman?" I asked. "Sherman Baxter?"

"Baxter Sherman," July said, peering at the screen. "He's one of five people on the email." She rose from the couch and headed toward her desk. "We should start downloading these emails."

"Okay," Frankie said. "But downloading stuff, I don't know."

"You don't know?" I said. "What don't you know?"

"You know," he said, shrugging.

"Frankie," I said, slowly and carefully, "now is not the time to be a morose teenager. Please be more precise."

"No need to condescend to me, Councilmember," Frankie muttered.

"Frankie, don't be an asshole," July said. She turned to me. "What he means is that if we save a copy of the files we may trigger some kind of security—"

"You save it, they find you," Frankie said.

"But not always," July replied. She pulled out her purse and began digging inside.

I looked at my watch. We'd been mucking around in their system for forty-five minutes. "Not always? What? What does that mean, 'not always'?"

"Some of the time," July said. "It's hard to say." July pulled her wallet out of her purse, then her makeup bag and her tablet. "Where the fuck is it?" she stammered.

I turned my back to Frankie, remembering why I wasn't a mother, and addressed July in a whisper. "We need these memos. Without them there's nothing to corroborate Billy's story that his supervisor squelched the accident report."

"It's a risk," July said, removing an umbrella from her bag.

"How big?" I asked.

She craned her neck to look around me at Frankie, sulking over the keyboard. I moved aside. "Hey," she said to him. "What are the chances we get busted if we save some files?"

"Twenty-four percent," Frankie responded.

"Voila!" July said, producing a thumb drive from the bottom of her purse.

It was pink, of course, meant to look like a cartoon character of some sort. She pulled a bit of lint off the creature's nose - probably a bit of swag foisted upon her by a constituent. She grimaced at me in apology.

"Twenty-four percent is pretty specific, Frankie," I said.

"He's kidding," said July.

"More or less," he confirmed.

"So, then?" she said, holding up the thumb drive. I could see now that it wasn't a cartoon creature but rather a thumb. A pink cartoon thumb with a manicured nail in deeper pink. July followed my gaze toward the thing. "New nail salon on Second Avenue," she informed me.

"Oh god, whatever," I replied. "Yes, just do it. Download the motherfucking memos."

She jammed the thumb into the USB port. "We'll finish reading the emails later," she said. "For now we need to just grab these memos and get off this network."

"Uh oh," Frankie said.

"Shit," said July. "It froze up."

"Yeah," Frankie said.

"What does that mean?" I asked.

"Probably nothing," July said.

"Right," said Frankie, "probably nothing."

"Probably?" I said.

"We should log off the site or do whatever you do now, Frankie," July said.

Do whatever you do? Why did July suddenly sound so clueless? And why was Frankie so frantically clicking the mouse if nothing were wrong?

"What's going on, you two?" I said. I crossed the room and looked at the laptop screen, expecting to find some kind of alert in big block letters: SECURITY BREACH. Instead, I saw a screen full of gobbledygook.

Frankie typed away at a frightening speed, ignoring us both.

July looked up at me and shrugged her shoulders.

"Okay," Frankie finally said. "We're good. No worries." He closed the laptop, stood from the couch, and handed it to July. "I'm out of here."

"Wait, what?" July said.

"Don't worry about all that," Frankie told her. He reached for his backpack. "You're golden. You got your files, right?"

"What was that all about, then?" I demanded. "What did you mean by 'uh-oh'? Why did the screen freeze up?"

Frankie turned to me for the first time since we entered the room an hour earlier and met my eye. "Because we got busted," he said calmly, and shrugged on his backpack.

"Excuse me?" I said.

"He's being melodramatic," July said.

"It was only the firewall," he said. "It's not like they're coming after you or anything."

"Explain, twerp," July demanded.

Frankie crammed a baseball cap onto his head and sighed like the irritating teenager he was turning out to be. What was I thinking, allowing July to bring an actual *child* into this scenario? The words *endangering the welfare of a minor* flew through my brain.

"All it means is that there's a record that somebody accessed the files. A little blip. They can't know who it was."

"Can they know which files were accessed?" I said.

Frankie looked at July, then bent to tie his shoe. When he got to the floor and realized his sneakers were fastened with Velcro, he tightened them instead. "Yeah," he said into the floor.

July and I stood there in silence, staring at one another.

"But they won't know we were there unless they look," Frankie said. "These little breaches happen all the time; nobody tracks this stuff down. They assume it's spam or bots."

"So, nobody will look? Nobody will care?" I ask.

"Basically, yeah," Frankie said, his hand on the door-knob. He looked like his life depended upon leaving the room, like he was about to die of social awkwardness. "We left a trail but we're the only ones who know it." He opened the door, ducked through it, and was gone.

"If we do nothing, stay quiet, we're fine," July said.

"How are you so sure? How do we know there isn't some kind of alert, warning them of a security breach?"

"Frankie might be weird, but he really does know his stuff," July said. "He's done bigger hacks than this, believe me."

"Great," I said. "Now we're dealing with a criminal."

I held up my palm. I didn't want to hear her response, which was surely going to have something to do with reminding me that our actions here tonight weren't exactly legal, either.

"Okay, let's assume Frankie the juvenile delinquent is correct," I said. "Nobody will come looking for us?"

"Not unless we give them a reason," July said.

"What kind of reason could we possibly give them?" I say aloud, and even as I say it I knew the answer. For what reason would they go looking for proof I'd hacked their system? If I were to go public with the contents of those memos, that's what. And, yet, we had the truth. We had proof of the cover-up. We knew what they were up to. But if we used our evidence, even if we leaked it to a third party and distanced ourselves, they'd investigate and find the breach.

"That laptop is registered to the campaign," I said, indicating with my chin the computer in July's hands.

She looked down at it, its brushed silver case glowing guiltily. "Shit," she said.

"At least tell me, please, that the files downloaded all right."

I watch July's face as she opens the thumb drive window. Everything fell. She slumped in her seat. "Nothing," she said. "Maybe the firewall stopped the download?"

"Please—" I say. She must be wrong. We didn't just leave a big slimy electronic slug trail running through the network of Regional Oil—a trail with my name on it—for no reason at all. She must be wrong.

I stood behind her and looked in disbelief at the screen containing the contents of July's pink thumb drive.

She was right. Nothing.

Chapter Twelve

I t's my mother's day to visit me in the slammer. We have a lot to discuss: her research on Regional Oil's safety record; Billy's intelligence gathering from work; my father's sciatica. My hair is all gone from the chemo but I've got the cute bob wig she bought me. It's a deep copper that she says makes me look a little dangerous. Yet in the scratched mirror over the toilet in my cell, my face is chalky, colorless. I look like someone stuck a wig on a fifty-year-old woman with cancer. I let Mercedes rub a little eyeliner and blush on my face.

When my name is called, I wait for the steel door of the visiting room to swing open and reveal my mother standing at her usual table, waiting for her hug.

But it isn't my mother standing there. It's my ex-husband, his hands hanging awkwardly at his sides.

"Tim," I say. I plaster a puzzled look on my face to cover the sudden rushing of my heart. I take three steps forward and halt uncertainly in front of him. Visitors are allowed two hugs, one upon arrival and one upon departure. My blood thumping and my ears full of the sound of crashing waves, I step forward and fall into his arms. At the smell of his neck, I feel a surge of comfort, as palpable as a breeze on my face. The chemo, the campaign, the trial: for three seconds it all goes away.

"Peg," he says into my ear, catching me subtly to avoid notice by the guard. He steadies me and pulls back to check my face. "Are you okay?"

"No long hugs," the guard says to the room in general and to us in particular.

I straighten myself—how would I get through that last chemo treatment if I still felt weak from the last one? I sit heavily on that damn molded plastic chair, attached to the table with its stupid iron arm that always bruises my knee. I am so sick of this chair. I am tired of the intense conversations happening in this chair. Also, the damn thing is uncomfortable.

I reach up to check my wig. Thank god for Mercedes and her eyeliner. Still, I know I look like shit.

"You look great," Tim says.

"Liar," I reply, smiling. "But it's nice of you to come."

"Funny," he says, "on the way over I nearly stopped to pick up a bunch of flowers."

"A reflex," I say, thinking of our old Thursday evening ritual, when he would bring home flowers, I would make martinis, and we would watch a movie.

"You had me trained."

"You loved it," I reply.

"You're right," he says and his smile was like a blue patch in a sky blank with clouds. I was utterly sunk. He was beautiful. He was magnificent. And I had so much unfinished business with him.

"Why did you come?" I ask him.

He looks away, at a spot over my shoulder. "I don't know, Peg," he says.

I watch his face. It hasn't changed much. He still carries his pain in his eyebrows, in the wrinkle of his forehead. "You wanted to say goodbye?" I say. "Before I go to jail for a decade or so?"

"Something like that," he says. He looks around the room, which is filled with other visitors and inmates, as if checking the location of the exits.

"Planning your escape?" I say, trying to be kind.

"I wanted to say I'm sorry," he blurts.

Oh Lord, is this what it's going to be like? Are people from my past going to start showing up, making speeches, making amends? Is this what happens when you get cancer and get sent to prison? Not that I wasn't thrilled to have Tim's apology, but it would have been nice to hear it *before* my life turned to shit. It would have been nice to know he wasn't apologizing out of pity.

"What for, Tim?" I say, trying to keep the impatience out of my voice.

"For cheating on you, of course," he says.

Here is where a decent human being would also confess her sins. A decent person would tell her ex-husband that at the same time he was fucking his cousin Rita's friend, she'd been fucking their insurance guy. But I'm about to go on trial and I'm sick as a dog from chemotherapy, so I give myself a pass on the decency thing. This apology is long overdue and there is so little that's going right in my life. I'm determined to savor the moment.

"I hope you'll forgive me," he continues. "I've been feeling shitty about this for the last couple of years and I couldn't stand the thought of you going to prison without knowing I'm sorry…"

"For the last couple of years?" I say.

"I know. I should have said this before—"

"No, it's okay," I tell him, realizing he's come to be absolved, as if I'm dying. How foolish I was to think he'd come because he misses me. Because we have unfinished business. Because he still loves me. "I forgive you," I tell him. "Of course I do."

I stand up, nod at the guard. More than anything I just want to leave the room.

"Peg, wait," Tim says, alarmed. "Where are you going?"

I glare at him. "Where do you think I'm going? Nowhere. I'm a prisoner."

"Why are you leaving, I mean," he says, reaching for my wrist and then pulling back. "Don't. Just. Hang on."

I pause. I just want to get back to my cell. "I hate that you're seeing me like this," I say.

"Peggy," he whispers.

"I'll take my hug," I tell him, and he unfolds himself from the chair and pulls me into his arms. He smells the same. It is too much comfort to bear, too much kindness, and I pull away without meeting his eye.

The guard opens the door and I leave Tim there, without looking back. On my way to my cell I imagine him still standing there, arms empty, watching me go.

Chapter Thirteen

During her jail visits, my mother has been unwilling to discuss the Glass Family Strategy. Meetings continue, she tells me, in my absence: my sister Tina, my brother Billy, my cranky father, his crankier father, and her, my mother, holding them all together. The five of them, giving over their Sunday suppers to conversations about how to save the ass of yours truly.

My mother has been an unshakeable ally my whole life, even when she disagrees—as she often does—with my viewpoints. My mom is why I'm a politician. She's the woman who raised me with feminist values, even though she'd never in a thousand years claim that term. She's one of those ladies who start a sentence with *I'm not a feminist, but...* followed by some extremely feminist idea.

At our last jail visit, she revealed a facet of their plan to bring me up to speed at a Glass Family Strategy Meeting with the whole family present.

"I'm in jail, Mom," I said. "They don't just let you out for Sunday dinner."

"I'm talking about a different location," she said. She spoke in a weird little whisper, from the side of her mouth. Her eyes flicked furtively around the room.

"You're really bad at this, Mom," I said.

"Worse things have been said about me," she replied.

They'd come up with an elegantly simple plan. Every time I've gone in for chemo, the jail guard sits outside the door and I go inside. I'm not allowed visitors but the other patients have theirs, of course, and we're all basically in the same room. So the family arranged Billy's chemo appointment to begin forty-five minutes before mine. When I get there, the Glass Family will already be present. This plan has been helped along, of course, by the warm relationship my mother has cultivated with the chemo nurses during her visits with Billy these past several weeks, as well as the fact that one of them had been her sorority sister back in the 80's.

But when my escort and I arrive for my last chemo treatment/Glass family meeting, my guard doesn't take his seat outside the door. Before I know what's happening, he's opening the door of the treatment unit and waltzing right inside.

When I walk in, just behind the guard, Tina comes loping toward me, hands outstretched. The guard is looking away from her, searching for the duty nurse.

Pinkwashed

Now this guy also works shifts as a waiting room guard in the jail. He's seen my family members before. The guards look pretty hard at people's faces.

Mid-stride, Tina's eyes take in the situation—my panicked face telling her to back away—and in that instant the guard turns toward Tina, toward this lady with a big wide grin coming across the linoleum, intent on a hug. Cringing, I watch Tina veer rapidly off-course, as though drunk, and embrace an elderly man standing placidly in the hallway, looking at his cell phone.

"Mordechai!" she cries. "Whatever are you doing here?"

The guard turns away. The confused old man is being hugged ferociously by my sister. At the far end of the room, I catch a glimpse of my mother, subtly drawing the curtain around Billy's bed, hiding the others grouped around him.

My sister widens her eyes at me.

"*Mordechai?*" I mouth at her, and she covers her mouth to hold the laughter, but is only partially successful.

Again the guard turns to look at her. Now recognition flickers across his face. Shit, I think, we're totally busted.

"Sir," says the chemo nurse. Her nametag says JUDY. "You can't be in here."

"Excuse me?" says the guard, turning his full attention to this woman's insubordinate attitude. This guard is not one of the nice ones—not that there are too many nice ones. This guy is just your basic bean brain jerk. "I'm a corrections officer, ma'am," he proclaims. "This here is my prisoner."

Judy takes a step toward his beefy belly. She holds up a clipboard containing a densely printed form. "And this here is what we call HIPAA. Once you cross this threshold, your prisoner is also our patient and, as such, she's entitled to her privacy. You, sir, are entitled to sit outside in a folding chair. Is that clear?"

Red-faced, the guard sputters a stream of words at her. She stands with her hands crossed and the clipboard across her chest. As the guard fumbles for his phone to call his supervisor, another nurse takes my elbow and leads me to the treatment station adjacent to the one where my family waits silently behind the curtain. Efficiently, Judy ushers my captor out of the room.

Before the meeting can begin, my chemo treatment needs to get underway. Billy is already half an hour into his drip.

"By the time this meeting gets started," Billy says, "the two of us are going to be sick as hell and barfing up bile."

"Thanks, bro," I say. And he's right, this meeting is going to be brutal. Since Billy's cancer is so aggressive he's on a longer schedule than me and his dosages more intense.

"He's right," my grandfather says. "Let's get this thing moving."

"Well, then," my mother says, "I'll call the meeting to order."

"Seriously?" I say. "You're using Robert's Rules?"

"Your mother has become quite the parliamentarian," my father informs me.

"It's about respecting the process, Fred," my mother says.

"You'll note I'm no longer running the family meetings, sweetheart," my father says.

Billy turns to me, whispering. "He didn't respect the process. He was disempowered by the new egalitarian thing we've got going here."

"That'll be enough from the two of you," my mother interrupts.

"I go away to jail for a few weeks and suddenly you're using collective decision making?" I'm dumbstruck. My family has always been a monarchy, my father in charge and, before that, my grandfather. Now he's leaning back in the visitor's chair with an expectant and resolved expression on his face, waiting for my mother to take the lead. I look at Tina for help. What's become of these people?

"Haters gonna hate," Tina says, shrugging her shoulders.

"What the heck does that have to do with anything?" my mother demands. Clearly, her new leadership role is wearing on her.

"A little joke, Mom. Just trying to diffuse the tension."

"What tension?" my mother says. "Never mind. Let's get started."

The Glass Family strategy, it turns out, is to draw media attention away from my misdeeds by shining a light on the misdeeds of the company instead. They, too, have been meeting with Ophelia. They therefore know that her fallback strategy—in case we fail to cast sufficient doubt upon the testimony of July and Frankie or if the State's case against me otherwise proves too strong and it's clear we're going to lose—is to argue for the moral righteousness of what I did. It won't change the verdict but if it turns out that my actions, illegal though they were, uncover corporate misdeeds, we dramatically increase my chances of a lighter sentence. The public loves a whistleblower, especially one who risks everything to blow her whistle. But only if she turns out to be right.

So my family has set out to prove me right. And this week there is progress to report. "You go first, Billy," my mother says, stroking his forehead with a cool towel as he begins to sweat, "Tell your sister what you found out."

"Six months before the fuel tank exploded, the state inspector cancelled his visit to the well site and he never officially came back," Billy says. "J. C. Vanderpelt—the guy who wrote the memo you read—told me he'd raised the alarm on that tank twice. He knew it was a hazard."

"Why did they cancel the inspection?" I ask. "And what do you mean by 'officially'?"

"This one, she needs all the answers all at once!" my grandfather says.

"We don't know details yet, Peg," my mother says. "We only just got this information."

"This is nothing new," my father says. "We all know the state doesn't have the inspectors. These things are cancelled all the time. I'd bet less than a third of the wells in the state get their annual inspections."

My mother leafs through a file crammed with papers. "You'd be right, honey. It's twenty-three percent, actually."

"So this is a systemic problem," I point out. "It's not about Regional Oil influencing the inspector, for example, or buying him off."

"Except this particular inspection, as it turns out, actually did happen," Billy affirms.

"He never came back *officially*," my grandfather interjects. "But he did eventually keep that appointment, am I right?"

"That's what Vanderpelt tells me," Billy says. "He said the inspector came, failed the site on the grounds of that faulty fuel storage tank, and cited the company an infringement that came with a fifty-thousand dollar fine.

"The fine isn't the issue," Billy emphasizes. "It's that infringement."

"Let me guess," I say, "that report disappeared."

"I can't find any trace of it and I've searched all the public records," my mother notes. "There are plenty of infringement reports online; just not that one."

"So now we're talking about corruption at the inspector general's office," my grandfather observes. "That's an elected seat, isn't it?"

We all fall silent.

"You all know who the state mines inspector is, right?" I finally say. All my family's eyes are on me.

My stomach starts to feel the effects of the chemo and I reach for the plastic bin. Up comes the half piece of toast I choked down for breakfast. My mother steps forward, stands between me and the others, and wipes my forehead. Here she is, two children with the same disease. It must feel to her like when we were young and sharing chicken pox, with our big sister standing in the doorway of the sickroom afraid she'd be next.

When my stomach stops its spasm and the nausea gives me a break long enough to speak again, I look up at Tina, who has her phone in her hand. She's showing the screen to my father.

"You just googled it," I say.

"Yeah," she replies.

"Benito Bennigan is the state mines inspector?" my father asks. "Holy shit, when did this happen?"

"About six months ago," I tell him. "He was appointed to serve out the rest of the term after what's-his-name's-heart attack."

"Right. Nobody ever remembers the name of the mines inspector," Billy informs them.

"Not this time. This name we recall," says my mother.

Benito Bennigan is the retired chair of the Greenville Republican Party and a fundraising powerhouse. Benito Bennigan emerged from his mother's womb straight into a backroom of old boys, smoking a cigar, pinching the ass of his waitress, and demanding she bring him a plate of rare prime rib.

"I wish you'd been able to get copies of those emails, Peg," Billy says.

By this time my family knew the truth. All of it. Three weeks ago, the evening before I went to the precinct with Ophelia to turn myself in, we had Sunday dinner together. I told them everything about that night with July and Frankie.

"Me too, brother," I murmur. "You have no idea."

"They'd have been inadmissible anyway," my mother says, snapping us out of our gloom. "No use crying over spilt milk."

"They would have been useful for clues," Billy laments. "If I could examine them, I'd know who knew what, and I could have—"

At the distressed look on my mother's face, Tina interrupts. "Okay, then, let's talk about Mercedes' grandma."

"Excellent, sweetie," my mother says. "Give us your report."

"You've been in touch with Mrs. Quinto?" I ask.

"They're best buddies now," my grandfather jokes.

"What can I say," Tina confesses. "She likes me."

"That makes one of us," I say.

"Yeah, she's not that impressed with you," Tina replies. "Frankly, I had to do some damage control."

Whatever! As a politician, I was hardened regarding others' opinions about me. It wasn't exactly a new experience for me to be disliked. Yet I wasn't about to thank my sister again for jumping in to play the good cop.

"Well done," I tell her instead. She needs the personal validation. Unlike me, she cares entirely too much what people think.

Properly recognized for her inherent goodness, Tina smiles to herself and continues. "Alma. Her name is

Alma," Tina says. "And despite her general dislike for you, she does believe you're the best hope for exposing the company. Ever since your meeting in the jail, she's been listening more closely to the ladies in the locker room."

"And what has she heard? What have they said about the tank explosion?" asks Billy.

"Nothing. Alma says they talk continually about business. About every little aspect, every meeting, every email. She says they never stop talking about work. She says they're obsessed, that they're not real human beings, that they don't have husbands or children or even friends. All they do is talk about profit margins and politics. In fact, I've got to say, Alma is a little obsessed by the obsession of these women."

"Cold-hearted bitches," utters my grandfather.

"Grandpa!" We women protest en masse.

"Sorry. I'm a sexist old fuck. What can I say?"

Tina continues. "Anyway, it's entirely possible they're not talking about the explosion except behind closed doors. But Alma doesn't think so. It seems to her they don't filter themselves at all. They talk about other things, equally reprehensible."

Tina consults her notepad, checking items off her list as she reports them to us. "They talk about screwing employees out of their workers' comp. They talk about reducing salaries so they can cover executive bonuses. They talk about their relationship with Senator McCray, a lot."

"Really?" I say. "And what do they say about McCray?"

Tina grins at me devilishly. Oh my, despite her irritating goody-two-shoes personality, I really do admire my sister. "You're going to love this," she says. "Or maybe hate it."

"Sounds about right. Try me."

"They're angling to put Boswell in the Senate."

"What the actual fuck," says my brother.

"McCray is retiring," Tina speculates.

"Yes," I tell them. The campaign had heard the rumors. "McCray will do it in midterm, which means no election for his seat. Someone will be appointed to complete his term."

"Same strategy they used for the mines inspector," mom says.

"Boswell," blurts my sister. "They're looking to appoint Boswell."

My brother takes this opportunity to vomit into his little plastic bowl. We all politely look away.

"Who makes senate appointments?" my father asks.

"The governor," I tell them. "We're screwed. He follows orders from the Republican leadership."

"Yeah," Tina confirms. "The ladies in the locker room pretty much have that Senate seat in their back pockets. This has been their plan all along. To put Boswell in the Senate."

"But only if Boswell won the election, is my guess," I say. "Otherwise it would've been dicey to appoint a guy with no actual experience."

My mother looks stunned. "Boswell is using your city council seat as a stepping stone! He's known from the beginning he wouldn't keep the job!"

My father has been quiet during Tina's speech and our dissection of this news. "You know, I'm thinking about those emails," he says. "The emails Peg read that night, about the explosion cover-up."

"It's no use—" interrupts my mother. "Let's stay on topic, dear."

Holding up his palm, my father says, "Hang on, now, sweetheart, I'm just wondering. They know it was you who hacked into their system, right Peg? They know which files you were accessing, too. Don't they? You were charged with the theft of proprietary corporate information, so that means they must also know what information you were trying to steal."

"Yes, Daddy," I reply patiently. I am getting ready to barf again. Billy's face is utterly white. He hasn't spoken for ten minutes. My mother is stroking his hair.

"But do they know you weren't successful?" asks my father. "Do they know that July's thumb thingy didn't work? Is it possible they don't know we don't have copies of those emails? Is it possible that they may think we know more than we do?"

We all turn to stare at him. "Yes, Dad," I say, wondering why this hadn't occurred to me before. "That is, in fact, entirely possible."

Chapter Fourteen

It took a while before July and I discovered why we hadn't been able to download those emails.

I was getting ready to deliver my stump speech at a fundraising house party at the sprawling mansion of Arnold O'Connor, CEO of United Wind Energy. His house was located in the fancier section of the already-posh East Greenville. This was the kind of neighborhood that doesn't get too many neighbors complaining about flammable water and dead farm animals. The social outrage here was more theoretical than immediate.

I was mid-sentence with the brother-in-law of our host—a personal injury lawyer with considerable potential as a major donor to the campaign—when July pulled me aside.

She ushered me into the powder room and told me what had happened. She had just pulled that same damn pink thumb drive out of her purse and tried to copy a file. She discovered the device didn't work, which was probably why we couldn't download those files.

"Are you saying it's possible that Regional Oil's cyber security did not actually catch onto us?" I whispered.

"Maybe," July said. "Maybe. Maybe if we'd downloaded the emails, it would have triggered something. Maybe we got lucky."

"That's a lot of maybes, July," I said.

"The problem is we don't know what we're talking about," she said. "We need to talk to Frankie." Frankie had gone completely silent on us. He wasn't responding to communication of any kind, which was freaking me out.

"No, *you* need to talk to Frankie. Figure this out, July. Find out how exposed we are. And for god sakes, keep me out of it. By the way, what makes you think he'll talk to you?" I asked.

"I'll find him. I won't give him a choice," July said.

"Now you sound like some kind of thug," I told her.

"Actually, I was just thinking I'd wait for him outside the high school."

"Now you sound creepy. Like I said, keep me out of it. Just pick his nerdy little brain and find out how seriously we're screwed."

She checked her watch. "School's out soon," July said. "I'm outta here."

When I turned to head down the marble-tiled corridor of the O'Connor living room, the host himself appeared, emerging from a side door and accompanied by a tall man bent over his phone whose face I couldn't see. Yet he seemed familiar.

From the other end of the corridor came my host's booming voice. "Councilmember!"

Arnold O'Connor was neither a small man nor a quiet one. Neither was he particularly attractive nor well dressed. For a corporate CEO, his social skills were seriously underdeveloped. He'd taken over the family business from his mother, who was a pioneer in the state's alternative energy industry.

"We've been looking for you!" he said. "It's time for the dogs and ponies." He held out his palm in guidance, poised to rest it at the small of my back. As if I needed help finding my way to his living room.

The man with the phone raised his head. My breath caught. It was Tim.

"How's your mom?" Arnold yelled into my face, despite his head roughly eighteen inches from mine.

"Uh," I said. What was Tim doing here?

"What?" Arnold replied. A head taller, Tim stood at his side. He wore a grin I remembered, a grin that made me feel on the inside of a secret.

"She's doing great," I managed to say, trying and certainly failing to keep my expression unreadable. Tim looked ridiculously handsome. And definitely older.

But then again, I'm older too.

"This here is Tim Johns," Arnold said, jerking his head toward my tall ex.

"We've met," Tim said, leaning forward and extending his hand. His palm was warm and dry and felt like a home I used to know.

"Well," Arnold said, oblivious to the electricity in the air, "you give her my regards, will you?" Arnold's mother and my mother had been in sixth grade together. Although it makes no sense demographically, it often seems to me that my mother attended school with half the population of Greenville.

"Shall we?" Arnold said. We stepped down the marble corridor toward his sitting room, where twenty major donors sat waiting. I felt Tim's presence at my side like a campfire warming one side of my body.

"What are you doing here?" I whispered to Tim. It had been well over six years since I saw him last, that night at Rita's house when I screamed at him through the front door. The next afternoon while I was at work he came to the house and took his things. The divorce papers arrived a month later. I signed them and that was that.

"Just supporting my candidate," Tim replied, a public smile plastered on his face as we stepped through the living room door to a burst of applause. Tim faded away as Arnold began a longish introduction of me that focused mostly on himself, somehow presenting my qualifications and commitments as evidence of his own wisdom and foresight.

As Arnold spoke, I tried not to make eye contact with Tim, who had placed himself at the back of the room and directly in my line of sight. On our wedding day, I remember thinking to myself, *this man is going to age well.* Looking now at his grizzled jawline and playful eyes, I see that I was right.

True, Tim cheated on me. Still, I was no victim. I was the coward. I had a lover, too. Yet, unlike Tim, I had the luxury of secrecy. He never found out and neither did anyone else. The affair ended shortly after Tim left me. I haven't seen the guy since. If Tim hadn't left so abruptly, if we would have had time to fight it out, to scream a little, to say what we had to say, I might have told him.

I like to think at least I would have told him. In terms of wrongdoing, I like to think I would have done Tim the courtesy of leaving him on more equal footing. He left without a word, though, and I was so angry. The divorce papers came and I heard he'd moved in with Rita's best friend. So what was the point? I let it go and let everyone around me believe I left my husband because he had an affair. I admitted my guilt to nobody.

These were my thoughts as I gave my stump speech. The great thing about stump speeches is that you can deliver them without having to concentrate on what you're saying. I opened by telling the crowd about my personal history as a native Greenvillian—although I've been around so long that everyone knows the story anyway—then about my position on raising taxes for education (yes), relaxing oversight on liquor licenses (no) and increasing small business subsidies (yes). As I spoke, I tried not to make eye contact with Tim. What was he doing here, anyway, both in Greenville and at this particular event?

I launched into the fracking section of my speech. After that day of fracking horror stories that July and I endured, we changed this part of my talk. I told these high-end donors about the man separated from his baby grandson because of fracking. I told the story about the chicken lady. Audiences love this shit. There's a reason that speechwriters for Presidents will stick the tribulations of some random dude from Arkansas within a speech. To really understand a situation, the human brain needs a story.

Then my human brain remembered the story of Tim's mother. When he and I split up, she'd just been diagnosed with Alzheimer's. Tim was devastated. He and his mother were very close. She raised him alone after his father left. I wondered if this was why he was back in town. Yet surely he'd been back many times to see her after our breakup so many years ago. Why was he showing up here now?

A woman perched on one of Arnold's overstuffed armchairs had been leaning forward for the past several minutes as though she had something to say. I'd never seen her before. She was middle-aged like me, dressed in a white summer sundress, her hair pinned at the top of her head. Her hand was raised even though the question and answer portion of the presentation was still minutes away. I hadn't yet gotten to the part of my speech having to do with the necessity of experienced leadership and the value of developed relationships. Also remaining was the story about the construction of the new gym over at Greenville High School and how my longevity in office had prevented an unscrupulous contractor from ripping off the school district. This lady, though, was determined to say something. I could see she wasn't going to wait for the Q and A. So, I interrupted myself to ask if she had a question.

"Not so much a question as an observation," she said. Inwardly, I groaned. People who start with the "not-so-much-a-question" opening are pretty much warning they're about to bore everybody in the room with an irrelevant, long-winded opinion.

"Until four months ago," she said, "I worked in public relations for Regional Oil."

"Really," I said. This was unexpected.

"I left when they asked me to lie on a press release."

A snort came from the back of the room. The woman turned around as if to address the snorter. "Yeah, okay, I know," she said. "What else is new? Stretching the truth is normal in public relations. We're all professional liars. Right? Right!"

I was dying to ask about the nature of the lie they wanted this woman to tell. I searched the room for July—to signal to her she should remind me to find this woman later and see how much she knows. Then I remembered she left the party to hunt down our incompetent hacker.

"Anyway," the woman was saying. "My point is that you'll never win."

"Hang on there, Maria—" interrupted Arnold.

"Sorry!" Maria said. "I didn't mean *you*, Councilmember. You'll totally win. We all know that." The room burst into a pleasant and gentle applause. "What I mean is you'll never beat Regional Oil." She paused and corrected herself. "No, what I meant is that *we'll* never beat them. We're not even playing on the same field."

"Well, you got that right," I said. "The resources alone. Compare their PR budget with my campaign budget, for example—"

"Yes," she said, "but that's not my point. My point is that they're liars."

Arnold inhaled, preparing to boom some opinion at her. Before he could interrupt, Maria raised her voice and continued. "We're not playing on the same field. That's true. It's because we're not even playing the same game. We think we are yet we aren't. They have their own set of rules. Secret rules."

Normally, when someone at an event starts talking about secrets and conspiracies, the staff member accompanying me will creatively interrupt the situation. July is especially good at shutting down the crazies, in the most polite way possible, to relieve me of the awkward burden of dealing with a nutcase. Unfortunately, July wasn't in the room.

Apparently realizing I was unstaffed, Arnold clumsily broke in. Although Maria was eighteen inches from his elbow and hadn't actually asked a question, Arnold shouted, "Great question, Maria!" He turned back to me and plowed on. "Can you tell us, Councilmember about your current approach to curbing the excesses at Regional Oil?"

"I'd like to ask Maria a question, actually," I said to Arnold, and not waiting for his response, I said to this woman, "can you meet me for a drink later on?"

Now the applause was more vigorous, more appreciative. It was also less polite, hungrier. Like me, the crowd had smelled blood.

At the cocktail reception afterwards, the woman gave me her name and number and then disappeared. The groupies, however, descended. The moment they did, Arnold approached and began describing a brand new campaign fundraising strategy he insisted would be effective, despite having no experience whatsoever in the field. Why must business executives continue to believe their limited experience transcends professions?

Thankfully, my phone rang.

It was Tim. "Hello there," he said. "Don't turn around."

It was our old routine. The thing he used to do when we were married, when I was first elected, and the pressure of my first term was so intense. I'd get caught in these dreadful conversations and, afterward, come home and scream at Tim all the things I wished I'd have said to whatever blowhard was mansplaining to me.

"Oh no," I said. This too was part of the routine. My phony reaction to some fake bad news coming over the phone.

"You remember," he said. "I'm flattered. By the way I'm outside, standing in this dude's actual private parking lot. White lines and everything."

"Of course, yes," I replied. I looked at my watch. "I'll be there in fifteen minutes." I turned to Arnold. "Fire needs putting out down at headquarters. I've got to go."

I thanked him for the lovely gathering and left him in his opulent living room.

In the parking lot, Tim was leaning against the passenger side of my car. He took my arm and stood close, stepped into my space. He dipped his head down toward mine and before I knew it we were kissing.

It was good. His mouth was both familiar and new. His hands landed on my hips exactly the way they'd always done. My purse slipped off my shoulder and landed with a *thunk* on the asphalt. I imagined Arnold peering from his living room window, watching his candidate making out with the stranger who showed up at his fundraiser.

Tim took the car keys from my hand and held the door open for me. I slipped in. When we were first married he hated driving and insisted I be the one behind the wheel. But when I started in politics and it became evident how much work needed to be done in transit— basically, he realized how many phone calls I was making as I drove, he took over the duties for the sake of safety. I loved him for it because it gave me more time to do my job. Ultimately, I used that job as an excuse to neglect him.

At the bottom of Arnold's long driveway, I said, "What about your car?"

"I'll come back for it later. I have a feeling Arnold will keep it safe for me."

"Where are we going?" I asked.

"Your place?"

Our old place. The house where we lived, together, for almost seven years. The house he left me in.

"No," I said.

He turned his head and looked into my eyes. "Right," he said.

"Where are you staying?" I asked.

"At my mother's."

"Well, *that* won't do," I replied.

"No," he agreed. "That won't do at all." He turned the wheel at a dirt road that suddenly emerged on the right, drove a hundred feet from the road, pulled the car sloppily to the shoulder and had our seatbelts unbuckled before I could even breathe.

I'd forgotten Tim's sexual urgency. It was like being married to a wolf, a strong, sexy wolf whose desire for you was boundless and intoxicating. His kiss left me dizzy.

He took my hand and placed it firmly at his crotch and moaned when I traced the outline of his stiffness with my thumb and index finger.

"Still ready, I see," I said.

"For you I'm always ready," he told me.

He pulled away. He leaned against the window and looked hard at me. I felt like a smiling, panting mess. Why had I let this man go? What had I been thinking?

"What is it?" I said.

"Hang on," he told me, and he opened the door and stepped outside. The sun had set maybe half an hour before. The sky was a deepening purple. Tim walked around the front of the car to the passenger side, opened my door and held out his hand gallantly for me.

I took it and he pulled me toward the front of the car. Among the crickets and lightening bugs, we pulled off our clothes. He lowered me with great gentle tenderness to the hood of the car, where we re-introduced ourselves in a way that wasn't so much gentle as terribly and wonderfully rough.

It wasn't until we were done, in my car on the way back to Arnold's parking lot, to pick up Tim's car, my hand on his thigh as he drove, that I remembered I'd sent July to find Frankie-the-hacker and that she hadn't returned to the party. What had happened? Where the hell was July?

Chapter Fifteen

By the time July comes back to visit me in jail, my trial is only days away. I'm glad to have Ophelia's blessing to see her but I'd have done so regardless. The boredom of jail makes you welcome any kind of human interaction, even the kind that's bad for you. And I could certainly use something to distract me from the effects of the cancer-eating poison coursing through my body. I feel like shit: weak, feeble, nauseous and bone-tired. Everything aches.

I've been thinking quite a lot about the day of the fundraiser at Arnold O'Connor's house. I never got the chance to debrief with July after she left to chase down our teenaged hacker. After my distracting detour into the woods with Tim, I went home and worked on campaign stuff, writing the text for a final hour get-out-the-vote robo-call. Pondering why we put up with robotic phone calls at all and considering everybody hates them, I fell asleep with my head on the table.

Imagine! This was only two weeks ago.

That night, rather than pondering irritating fundraising strategies, I should have been pondering the whereabouts of July. Election Day was approaching. By this point, in any election, you're joined at the hip with your campaign manager. So it was strange that she was out of touch. When I woke up at 3 AM and peeled my face from the kitchen table, I checked my messages again. Nothing from July. Why hadn't she checked in to update me on the status of that stupid pink thumb?

When the guard comes to the cell and informs me I have a visitor, I am expecting to see Ophelia. She said she'd be coming by to update me on my case. Last time she came, she spoke more about my public image than anything else, saying with her silence what we both already know—that I'm going to lose this case. At this point, the question is to what degree. I am charged with election fraud, which carries a minimum sentence of six months and a maximum of three years.

Once again, my guess was off. My visitor wasn't Ophelia but July.

"You realize the prosecutor would birth a cow if he knew you were here," I tell her, without saying hello. I can practically hear the creak of my bones as I sit down.

"His mood would be the least of my problems," July replies. "I'm pretty sure this visit puts me in contempt of court."

"Then it must be important," I observe.

"Your trial is next week," she says.

"Really?" I say. "I wasn't aware." My head is killing me. I'm a few days from my last chemo treatment and have never felt more grateful for anything in my life. Still, as awful as chemo has been, my cancer isn't exactly the heavy-duty kind. After a certain age we're all playing an awful game of cancer roulette. Every day I'm aware I'm getting off easy. My brother? Not so much. I can hardly think about his disease. The ache is too sharp.

"Okay, Peg," July says. "I get it. You don't trust me."

The night July went AWOL, I should have known things were going badly. But would I have behaved differently? Would I have called off the campaign if I had known just days before the election what July found out that night—that we were screwed? It turned out that our hopes for the faulty thumb drive were pitifully baseless. When July cornered Frankie outside the school, he admitted he was "pretty sure" that Regional Oil had likely traced the IP address of the campaign's laptop, not that I learned any of this from July. She showed up at the campaign office the next morning, claiming she couldn't find Frankie anywhere. This came out later, in my hearing.

"Why did you lie to me about seeing Frankie that afternoon?" I asked. "What did he say to you that you wouldn't tell me?" I think of Ophelia. She wouldn't be happy to know that I'm grilling her witness. But I'm still so confused about how I ended up where I am. July has answers and I'm going to get some.

At the table to our left sits a fellow prisoner and her daughter, a girl of nine or ten wearing a soccer uniform. The girl is absently kicking at the post underneath the table. Because our tables are connected via some sort of iron infrastructure, each time the kid kicks the post, my table shudders.

July is digging through her purse. She hasn't answered my questions about Frankie. All week long I've been either incapacitated by chemo or crazed with anxiety about the very real possibility I'll end up behind bars for a long time. Perched on the seat of my plastic chair and rubbing at the bruises from knocking my knees against this godforsaken visitor furniture, I watch July remove items from her handbag, looking for something. In addition to sending thudding vibrations through our tabletop, the kid next to me is also pulling at her hair and picking vigorously at a scab on her knee.

"Voila!" July says, and pulls out the famous thumb drive. She places it on the table between us, where it sits, pinkly.

"What the fuck, July," I say.

"No passing items to inmates," booms the security guard.

"Sorry!" July chirps, and puts the thumb drive back in her purse. She raises up her skinny white arms in a "hands up, don't shoot" gesture and smiles charmingly at the guard, who backs away. Beautiful people. It's astonishing the shit they get away with.

"What are you doing with that thing?" I hiss.

"Frankie was able to access the files," July tells me. "That night I went to see him. He did some kind of repair to the thumb drive and there they were. The memos, the emails. We got it all."

"Why the hell didn't you tell me?"

"Because of the other thing I learned that afternoon from Frankie," July says. She leans forward, her perfect blond hair brushing the tabletop. A little cloud of her subtle perfume wafts over me. "That afternoon, when I found him after school, I brought him back to my place and persuaded him to take another trip back into the Regional Oil network."

The girl next door has kept up an unsteady, arrhythmic beat with her foot against the table leg. She's a wreck, poor kid. Her mother's in jail and she's angry and embarrassed. I feel for her. Still, I'm about ready to grab her knee in a death grip to get her to stop kicking the goddamn table. My headache is reaching epic scale.

Suddenly, I'm certain she's setting me up. "Please don't say anything else," I say to July.

"I've taken a risk coming here." she says. "I have nothing to gain and everything to lose."

"Fine. But tell it to my lawyer."

"I can't and you know it," July says in an urgent whisper. "I'm going to tell you this whether you want to know or not. The truth is that Frankie found evidence that the Regional Oil tech guys knew we were there. In their network. I can't explain how right now. It's too complicated and I barely understand it myself."

"But the lawyers will understand," I say. "The judge will understand."

"Now you see why I couldn't tell you about the emails," July says.

"You thought you were reducing my exposure?" I hissed. "Are you kidding me?"

"Well I did, didn't I?" she says. "In fact, you never saw the emails at all, did you?"

The girl to my left has begun to cry and, as she does, her foot connects more firmly with each kick to the table leg. My headache has triggered a queasy upset in my stomach and my anti-nausea meds are back in my cell. I may just barf on the table. That would still this kid's foot for sure.

"What, you're telling me you took the fall for me?" I say.

"Not yet I haven't," July says.

"Excuse me?"

July leans back in her chair. The guard shouts that visits are over in five minutes. She takes a breath and then lets it loose. "I had an affair with Frankie when he was a sophomore in high school. I was his little sister's babysitter. We used to have sex after she was asleep. I was nineteen and he was fifteen."

"Oh for god's sake, July."

"Yes, I know. But listen."

"This could have taken down the entire campaign. My whole career—"

She's looking at me with an expression on her face that reminds me I've already managed to do all of that by myself, without any help from her.

"Okay, fine," I say. "Tell me why this matters. Why are you telling me this now?"

"Don't pretend that your defense isn't built entirely on destroying my credibility," she says. "And Frankie's."

"I can't talk about that," I say, fighting another wave of nausea.

"Whatever. The point is that you need to toss me under the bus, Peg."

I sit back in my plastic chair and close my eyes. I absorb what July is saying, what she's doing.

"You'll be charged with statutory rape," I say.

"None of us are emerging from this unscathed," she replies.

I feel chastened. My head is pounding. July fucked up but here she is, accepting the consequences. I suspected her unfairly.

"You shouldn't take the fall for me," I say.

"Sorry to bust your bubble, Councilmember, but I'm not doing this for you."

By this point the girl's foot is causing earthquake tremors to the table. Her mother looks at me apologetically. I can feel the woman's pain. Her kid is very close to a meltdown and asking her to stop kicking the furniture might just put her over the edge.

"I'm not doing this to keep you out of jail," July continues. "I'm doing it for Greenville. To wreck Regional Oil. To end fracking once and for all. We've got to get rid of those motherfuckers. Getting you back in office is the best way to do it."

"How will this help? Why should both of us go down?"

July looks at me like I'm a fool. Which of course is true.

"Because this is the only way we can get those emails into the record. Even if your lawyer wanted to introduce them, they'd get tossed out because they were obtained illegally. We need to help your lawyer convince the jury that you really knew nothing."

"But either way," I say, "the memos will be declared inadmissible because they were fucking *stolen*."

"Nothing is inadmissible in the court of public opinion," July says. "Inside the courtroom, we clear your name based on ignorance and based on my tawdry past with Frankie. Outside the courtroom, we work the media. We release the emails to the press, tomorrow."

"And what about you, July? Are you willing to go to jail for sex abuse?

"Don't forget election fraud," she says, with all the calm in the world. "But no, hell no. "I'm moving to Rome. Tonight. My suitcase is in the car."

"July!" I exclaim.

"Call me Julietta," she replies.

I am stunned. I knew this woman had moxie but holy shit.

"This is the plan we've come up with," she tells me, "and this is the plan we're using, whether you like it or not."

"We?" I say, as my headache delivers a particularly vicious throb.

"Your staff, Peg. Remember us? We've been meeting almost every night since you've been in jail, figuring out what to do."

"And this is the best idea you could come up with?" I say.

"You think you can do better?"

146

I've got to concede that I can't. Apart from wrecking July's career and turning her into an international criminal, this plan leaves the least amount of damage and gives us the best chance of defeating the frackers.

The girl next to us continues her thumping. I look down and realize she's wearing soccer cleats. No wonder the kicks are resonating so effectively. For the first time, July seems to notice the thumping that's been making me crazy. She leans across our table to the girl, rests her hand gently on her forearm. "Sweetie pie," July says, with a gentle and loving smile on her face. "Could you try maybe to keep your foot still? My friend isn't feeling so well today."

"Oops!" says the girl and offers July a shy smile. "Sorry."

Goddamn July. She always gets her way. Even from the wreckage of a career-ruining scandal, she manages to finagle a new life in Italy.

I think suddenly of my niece, whose mother hasn't allowed her to join the Glass Family meetings. "Does Jennifer know about this?" I ask.

July laughs out loud. "Does she know?" she says. "All of this was her idea. That girl has been chairing our meetings."

My sister told me that Jennifer was furious at having been excluded from our scheming. I should have known she wouldn't go away quietly. I am proud to bursting.

"Tell Jennifer she needs to talk to her mother and tell her what you're planning."

"I doubt that's going to happen," July responds. "Our committee is pretty damn secret."

"Another secret committee is operating too," I tell her. "It's time you joined forces."

July raises her eyebrows. "Well, that's good news. But, you'll have to tell her yourself. I'm on my way to the airport. As of now I've officially disappeared."

The guard is making the noises he makes when it's time to end the visiting period. Other visitors are standing to leave. The little girl with the busy foot smiles at July.

"Oh!" July says. "I almost forgot. The Fan Club."

"Those crazies," I murmur. I shift in my seat. Why does every bone in my body hurt so much?

"Hey," July says, reprimanding. "Those crazies might just save your ass."

"The Boland Run for Cancer Research is coming up, isn't it?" I say.

She nods. "And the Fan Club has decided to launch into full-on activist mode. You should see the costumes they've dreamed up."

"What?" I'm astonished. "Street theater?"

"They caught wind of the pink drill bits," says July, with an evil little grin on her face.

"Let me guess who told them," I say.

"Guess again," July says. "I wish I could take credit but that was all your niece's doing. She's been attending the Fan Club meetings, too."

"Do they know that Boland plans to reveal the drill bits at the terminus of the walk? That they're planning some kind of obnoxious PR party?"

"Oh, honey," says July, turning to leave, to disappear from my life forever, "they sure as heck do."

Chapter Sixteen

In my life as a politician, I've opened my morning paper on more occasions than I can count and learned news that made me scream. The morning after my reunion with Tim, I awoke to discover what July found out the night before and didn't have the courage to tell me. We'd been busted by the cyber security system at Regional Oil.

When July visited Frankie, she convinced him to try hacking Regional Oil again with the purpose of finding out whether we'd been caught the first time. Never mind that committing the same crime twice wasn't the smartest way to gather this information. In any case, Frankie encountered firewalls that hadn't been there before, a clear signal the company knew they'd been hacked. And if they knew they'd been hacked, they also knew by whom.

What July didn't know then was that the company had already been in touch with *The Greenville Star*. As she was sitting with Frankie, gaping incredulously at a screen that basically informed her we were deeply screwed, Janice Beachwood at *The Star* was hunched over a screen of her own, finishing up a story that was due to run in the morning edition. I read the headline even before I had had my coffee. *Regional Oil Hacked; Breach Points to Glass Campaign.*

Normally, scream-worthy headlines are a noisy affair. Sometimes my neighbor gets alarmed and knocks on my door. That day, however, my meltdown was more silent. I just went back to bed and screamed into my pillow.

When I finally made it to campaign headquarters, I encountered a somber mood. The team was waiting for me in the conference room. July was already there. She had given everyone the basic details of our recent indiscretion, saving me the humiliation of having to explain my stupid behavior to the people on my payroll.

"The article said they connected the hackers to an IP address registered to the campaign..." Jennifer was saying as I walked in. She let her voice trail off.

"Go on," I said.

The last thing I wanted to do was to make some kind of speech or, for that matter, to speak at all. Speaking was overrated. Speaking would only get me into trouble. For a moment I indulged myself in the fantasy that perhaps I could just carry on the rest of my campaign—in fact my whole political life—without speaking another word. Maybe I could get people to trust me simply by smiling benevolently at them.

Testing out my theory, I smiled benevolently at Jennifer. She looked at me like I'd gone mad. Maybe she was right. Maybe I was just a smiling crazy woman.

"Anyhow," Jennifer said, "which computer was it?"

"That doesn't matter," July said brusquely.

Jennifer cast me a look that told me she knew July was full of crap and that the computer in question mattered quite a lot.

"What I'd like to know," Dan said, "is how she can claim the campaign wasn't reachable for comment."

"Yesterday evening I was out of touch for maybe four hours," I said, trying not to blush. I turned off my phone while trysting with Tim. I was so distracted by his presence and my unexpected desire that I also hadn't even checked messages after the fundraiser at Arnold's. It was as though I'd forgotten I was running for office and that Election Day was around the corner.

"When I got home and looked at my phone, I found exactly two messages from Janice Beachwood, twenty minutes apart," I said. "They came in around eight o'clock, while I was working the crowd at Arnold's." By the time I listened to the messages—she didn't tell me why she was calling, only that she wanted a quote—it was after midnight, so I ignored them and worked on my robo call.

"She didn't try very hard to reach you," grumbled Dan.

"The question is whether we can recover," July said.

"Yes, that's exactly the question," I replied, eager to move the dialogue forward or, more accurately, in any direction that didn't involve talking about my monumental lapse in judgment.

Jennifer snorted. "That's hardly the question."

"Okay, Jennifer," said July. "That's enough."

"That's enough?" I said to July. I didn't like the way she was talking to my niece.

"I've been uppity," Jennifer said. "July wishes I'd just be quiet already."

"We've been talking about this for a while," Dan said. "We're all a little bit on edge."

The table was strewn with coffee cups and empty plates. A lone donut sat in the middle of a pink pastry box. I picked it up and took a bite, stalling. They all watched me chew. "The question," I finally said, "is how much caffeine and sugar have you guys consumed this morning?"

Nobody laughed. "Actually," Jennifer said, "the question is what the fuck were you doing in Regional Oil's computer system?"

"She's upset," Dan said.

"Quit speaking for me, Dan," Jennifer said.

"Jennifer, please," July said.

"Okay, everyone," I said. To my dismay, they all stopped talking and looked at me. Clearly, they were hungry for some kind of leadership. So, I opened my mouth and told them a bunch of baloney about survivability despite last minute scandal, about how the electorate looks upon these kinds of things with grave suspicion, about how anything coming out of Regional Oil these days is hardly taken seriously given their record, etcetera.

They knew I was bullshitting them. At the moment when all they needed was for me to deliver some clarity and direction, all I could do was turn on my politician's face and deliver them a bunch of smooth talk. I told myself I was protecting them. And, maybe I was. The less they knew, the better. Yet what if I had said, *Okay, guess what, I screwed up, I can't go into details. How can we fix this?* What if I had reached out to these people instead of shutting them down?

As I spoke, I watched their expressions change from expectant to disappointed. Jennifer's chin was trembling. Holding my eye, she interrupted my little speech by holding up her phone and shaking it in the air. "Aunt Peg?" she said, "I just got a text message."

"Yes, Jenny," I said, my patience thinning. "What is it?"

"It's from my grandmother," she said, the clever troublemaker. "She wants to know if you're going to jail. What should I tell her?"

We spent the next 24 hours dodging the press and, when we couldn't, we made vague statements. At every chance possible, we turned the conversation back to my opponent and his relationship with fracking.

That afternoon, the woman named Maria who'd shown up at Arnold's fundraiser—the one who'd worked in public relations for Regional Oil—appeared at campaign headquarters and volunteered what turned out to be her exceptional skills at writing press releases that say exactly nothing.

We used the words we needed to use. We finessed like a pack of tango champions. We were dancing around the flames of my career. When it came down to the actual question, a question finally pressed upon me by the despicable Janice Beechwood herself, whose skills at reaching me by phone became suddenly very acute—"Councilmember Glass, did you or did you not hack into the computer network at Regional Oil?"

"No," I said. "Absolutely not." In other words, I denied everything and lied my ass off.

As usual, our election night party was held at the Greenville Hilton and, as usual, the Repubs took over the Greenville Sheraton. If nothing else, we are parties of habit.

Our previous two days in damage control mode left us all frazzled. We were moving forward with the goal of getting me elected so I could bust Regional Oil for covering up the explosion and manipulating local democracy. Until then, we were spinning, hard. Down the line, I hoped these revelations about the company would clean my slate. I hoped that after I was elected the voters would forgive me for being a big fat thief. But mostly, just for the next few days, I hoped the voters would believe my lies. I was playing with fire, risking it all, and I knew it.

Despite their conservative leanings, my family has always shown up at Democratic HQ on election night. It's something of an annual tradition for my campaign volunteers to give them a good ribbing about bringing them over to the Dark Side Hilton, all very loving and respectful. The jokes never change and the sincere handshakes never weaken. None of my family has ever gone so far as to join me on the podium, however. Twelve years ago, on my first election night, my volunteer campaign chairman asked my parents to stand behind me onstage for the victory speech. "No thanks," my father told the man. "I'll be supportive but I won't be disingenuous."

They occupied their regular table up front next to the podium - my mom and dad, my brother and sister and their spouses and kids. In a last-minute burst of family loyalty, Jennifer took a seat between her parents.

It had only been a few weeks since the Glass Family Meetings had begun and Billy and I learned about one another's cancers. My mother showed up at my campaign headquarters the day before. July brought her back to my office, through the warren of cubicles filled with volunteers calling voters to remind them to get off their American butts tomorrow and exercise their right to vote.

"Thanks for returning my message," my mother said, closing the door to my office behind her.

There were two callers on hold, waiting to talk to me. One was the chair of my fundraising committee.

"Give me a break, Mom," I said. "It's been a little busy around here."

"Bullhockey," she replied. "When you're on the front page of the paper because someone's accused you of stealing, you're damn well required to call your mother to explain yourself."

"The election is tomorrow, Mom," I said. My cell phone vibrated noisily on my desk, "Seriously, I'm quite busy."

"And it never occurred to you that your family might be useful to you at a time like this?

"I appreciate the support, Mom. Thank you. I really do." I checked my watch. I was due to leave in twelve minutes to attend a last-minute, get-out-the-vote rally at the new supermarket that just opened on Route 1.

"I'm not talking about moral support, Peggy," my mother told me. "I'm talking about information. About progress on our project."

I was confused. "What?"

"If you know what I *mean*," my mother continued, obliquely.

"No, Mother, I don't know what you mean," I said, not bothering to hide my irritation. July was looking at me through the window in my office door with her eyebrows raised and finger-tapping at her wrist.

"Quit being obtuse, dear," my mother said. "You know what I mean. You also know it's best we don't talk about it over the phone. That's why I chased you down. So we can talk in person."

"Mom," I said helplessly, and gestured at the desk phone, at my cell phone, at July. "Look around. I can't talk now. Tomorrow, in case you hadn't noticed, is Election D—"

"Vanderpelt," my mother interrupted.

"Mom—"

"Vanderpelt has agreed to blow the whistle," she said, speaking quickly and quietly, looking me hard in the eye and using that serious mother voice, the one that works some kind of ancestral magic on your psyche and makes you pay attention.

"He'll go on record about the inspection report they asked him to squelch," my mother continued. "Everything. He'll corroborate Billy's story about the tank explosion, about the problems with the storage system beforehand, the problems he spotted and was told to ignore—"

July gave up waving at me through the window and opened the door. "We've got to go, Peg—" she said and then stopped talking, as I walked from behind my desk to envelop my mother in a hard and happy bear hug.

"He's at the newspaper office now," my mother said. "Talking to that reporter who hates you so much."

"You did it," I said into my mother's shoulder. I choked back a sob of relief.

"We all did," she whispers, stroking my hair. "But it was mostly your brother. It was Billy who convinced him to talk."

Sitting now at the Glass Family table on election night at the Hilton, my brother Billy looks like crap. As for me, the side effects of the chemo are turning my stomach into gelatin and making me sweat like an elephant. Billy's chemical cocktail is far stronger than mine. I can only imagine the discomfort he's feeling. I find a minute in the madness to sit with him.

"How go the numbers, sis?" he says. He pokes at the lime in his club soda.

"Same," I reply. "Waiting for the Fifth." The Fifth was District Five, Greenville's most densely Democratic area and, incidentally, also the most populous. Districts One, Two, and Four, all heavily Republican, had already reported their votes, as had the barely Democratic Sixth. The Third, which always reported last due to its rural setting, had so few constituents that their votes were statistically insignificant and always the last to be recorded.

Every election night in Greenville, this is how it went. In the early evening, the Republicans would be in the lead. As the night wore on, the Democrats' numbers would creep up—possibly enough, possibly not—until finally, when the results of the vote in the Fifth were announced, someone in the media would call the election. Blessedly, it would all be over for another election cycle.

"So, what's the spread?" he asked.

"They're seven points up," I replied.

"That seems like a lot."

"It's more than a little bit," I agreed.

"Will it work?" he said. "The Vanderpelt thing?"

"It's a last-minute surprise," I said. "Voters will be confused."

"Today's headline has got to help," he dryly observed. Indeed, it would.

Under the headline *Whistleblower at Regional Oil Spills Info on Cover-Up*, the front page of this morning's *Star* reported with admirable impartiality Vanderpelt's allegation that the executive leadership of Regional Oil, in collusion with the state mines inspector and former chair of the Greenville Republican Party, covered up an industrial accident that permanently disabled a worker and likely resulted in a long, slow leakage of fracking chemicals into Greenville Creek.

"The thing about the creek was a surprise," I said.

"That was Mom," Billy said. "She crunched some numbers on water quality in the creek before and after the tank exploded and gave the stats to Beachwood."

"Let me guess. They were footnoted."

"And annotated."

"That's how she rolls," I said. We grinned at each other for a good long moment. Then his eyes refocused to a spot over my shoulder.

"What's *she* doing here?" he said.

I turned and followed his gaze. The new volunteer, Maria, was standing at the edge of the room, halfway behind a potted plant. She was wearing some kind of loud floral hippie skirt and talking to a woman in a blue business suit whom I didn't recognize. "Who is it?" I asked Billy.

"I know her from the company," Billy said. "She's one of the execs."

"Why would she be talking to my PR volunteer?" I said.

"That's your PR volunteer?" Billy said, frowning. "Do you think she knows who she's talking to? Because that woman is the secretary in the public relations division at Regional Oil."

"You've got to be kidding me," I whispered. I looked around for July and found her coming my way with a puzzled look on her face. She'd spotted Maria and the mystery woman, too.

"Who's that person?" July asked, taking the seat on my other side.

The three of us watched them while pretending not to watch. "Billy says she works for Regional Oil. In the PR department."

"Damn," July said. She rose halfway from her chair. "Should I intervene?"

"No, hang on," I said. "Maria might be getting information."

"What's with that skirt?" July said.

"She sure doesn't dress that way at the office," Billy said. "Usually she's in a suit, like the other one."

July and I turned to look at him.

"What?" July said.

July and I looked at one another in confusion. Then we both looked again at Billy.

"What do you mean, what?" Billy said.

"Billy, dearheart," I finally said, "Exactly which one of those women is the secretary you're talking about?"

"The one in the hippie skirt," he said.

July and I met eyes and this time we laughed. The tension of the campaign had gotten to us all. Here we were, expecting spies behind every potted plant.

"You mean she *used* to work there," July said to Billy. "A while ago. Yes, we know. She's a bit of a secret agent."

"No," Billy said. "I mean she works there now. I saw her yesterday in the cafeteria. Her name is Maria. She's the executive assistant to the Vice President of Corporate Communications. She's worked at the company for like seven years. She has a poodle named Einstein."

Just then a bout of nausea washed over me. The oncologist told me this can happen in moments of stress. So, I ducked my head between my knees and Billy placed a supportive hand on my back and advised me to breathe.

"Maria's a double agent," I said. "We are so fucked."

Just then there came a cheer from the front of the room as the results for the Fifth District appeared on the jumbo screen.

The results were immense. They were enormous. They slid me over the top with four percentage points to spare. I gaped at the screen in shock.

I won.

We won.

My mother was grasping at my shoulders. My brother struggling to his feet to kiss me on the cheek. My niece

Chapter Seventeen

Topping the list of the many things I won't miss about being a politician is the ongoing and never-ending conversation about my wardrobe. A life in politics would have you accepting that what a woman wears matters more than what she says. Fighting this Neanderthal view of women in public service is a war without end and the battlefield, of course, is our bodies.

Unless there's something striking about a male politician's person, unless he's freakishly short or uncomfortably handsome or weirdly sloppy, unless he wears odd ties or never trims his beard, he's basically left alone when it comes to his appearance.

Women politicians, on the other hand, need wardrobe consultants. Mine is Ginny Weathermill, a ninety-year old retired bank manager, fashionista, and native-born Greenvillian. I was still in high school when Ginny retired from the bank and rented a storefront on Main Avenue. She opened Weathermill's and has spent the intervening twenty-five years surprising the women of Greenville by filling her store with an inventory that is unconventional and yet, somehow, exactly traditional.

Ginny and I have been through three campaigns together. When it comes to my clothing choices, she and I have a kind of dance. Ginny will present a certain very girly outfit with a flourish. I will refuse. She will say okay and show me something else. Then, Ginny will present the refused thing again. I will tell her no way, no way, stop asking me; she will say okay and show me something else, all the while holding tucked under her arm that first rejected outfit, as a sort of threat: *choose one of these outfits or else you'll end up in this girly thing*. Half the time, I'd choose something else and end up in the girly thing anyway.

It's an argument I cannot win because every time Ginny dresses me for a special occasion, people go a little bonkers over my outfit and I see a bump in the polls. Because of this infuriating fact, I both detest Ginny Weathermill and love her desperately.

The day before the trial Ginny appeared in the jail's waiting room with a selection of suits for me to wear on trial day. Predictably, the first one she showed me was pink. Dusty rose pink. The pink of a dead flower. The pink of a dead career. She held up the offending article for my inspection.

"Please," I whimpered. "No."

"Just kidding!" she chirped and zipped the thing back into its bag.

"That's not nice, Ginny," I said.

"Just warming you up," she replied. She unzipped the next bag and pulled out a sober black pantsuit that was so perfect I wanted to cry. It made a statement both serious and chic and communicated a sort of Jackie O style-amidst-tragedy look.

"It's exquisite," I said.

"Yes, I know," she replied, frowning at it.

"What?" I said. I didn't like the look on her face. I noticed then that the suit bag wasn't empty.

"It's up to you," Ginny said, reaching for the bag. "You need to know that right now. No strong-arming, no arguing—"

"You say that every time," I told her. I didn't want to see what else she had in the bag. I wanted the chic black pantsuit and nothing else.

Ginny paused and looked at me. "Well, let's get real, Peg," she said. "As we both know, it's rarely up to you. But not this time. This is something different, isn't it?"

Then she pulled a pantsuit out of her bag that was identical to the first except for the fact of a color of such a shocking bright pink that I was momentarily blinded. I covered my eyes in horror.

"Don't fuck with me, Ginny," I told her. "I'm weak from the chemo."

"Listen," she told me. "It's up to you. Everyone agrees."

"Everyone?"

"The team vetted these two suits," she said. "It took twelve people and four meetings."

"What statement exactly does the team believe is made by the pink one?"

Ginny inhaled. "Okay," she began. "As I'm sure you've noticed—"

"It's Boland Pink," I said.

"Right. The group thinks—"

"I need to reclaim pink," I said. "For women everywhere. I need to boldly drape myself in the color of the corporate overlords who have co-opted it. "

"You know your team," she said.

Of course I knew my team. I'm the one who trained them. "It's very good PR," I admitted. "A bit on the brilliant side."

"They knew you'd agree."

"I haven't agreed yet," I said grumpily.

"There's always the black," Ginny reminded me. "Nobody wants to make you do anything—"

"Oh yes they do," I said. "They always do. They're always wanting to make you do something you don't want to do. Something that makes you uncomfortable and irritated."

"That's where you're wrong," Ginny said gently. I looked up then, away from the suit and toward her eyes, and there I saw an old friend, the woman whose two hands have placed more clothes on my body than anyone, perhaps even my mother. This woman knows my measurements, knows my skin. Knows what looks good on me and what doesn't. "Everybody wants you to be well," she chided me. "Nobody wants you to feel silly. We need you at your best, at your most confident. We all agreed. If you can't embrace the pink— if you can't or if you won't, for whatever reason, no questions asked, no pressure, no nothing—you wear the black."

Now Ginny is sitting somewhere behind me in the courtroom, rocking a high-waisted, ivory dress with delicate chocolate embroidery at the hemline and a pillbox cap that seems to have come from some distant, more fashionable planet than our own. My heart surges with love for her.

Me, I'm wearing pink. Barbie Pink. Pepto-Bismol Pink. My suit is the pink that spills from the toy box of every girl in America who will one day grow up to look in the mirror at age twenty-five to wonder why, in some vague and inexplicable way, her life, her choices, her body, don't seem quite *pink* enough for the rest of the world. It is the pink cupcake frosting smeared on the paper tablecloth and left overnight to harden. It is the pink of the hula-hoop spun by your prettier rival in an unwinnable contest of endurance. It is the pink of unicorn farts.

I am wearing the shit out of this pink. I am *owning* this pink. I have so fully embodied this color pink that the beads of sweat on my forehead are infused with its tint. I am reclaiming this pink from those who would abuse it. I am making this pink my bitch. I am politicizing this pink. I have become a person of pink.

I'm wearing a brilliant white silk blouse under the jacket with a broad collar. Ginny has accessorized me in a single strand of pearls at the throat and high, white pointed pumps that pinch my toes. Still, there's no mistaking the intent of my pink power suit. Councilmember Glass will not take this shit lying down.

I turn my head, searching for Tim's face in the crowd, when the back door to the courtroom opens and in sweeps Sheila Maguire, the CEO of Regional Oil, accompanied by her entourage of locker room executives.

She sees me in my power suit and smirks. She turns to the executive on her left, a giraffe-like redhead in tiger-striped pumps whom I recognize as Eleanor Allison, her vice president of public relations. She whispers something to the group. Like a posse of high school mean girls, they all swivel their well-coiffed heads in my direction and smirk the same smirk as their ringleader. I know that such a corporate smirk is meant to communicate derision. I've learned something, however, from the times I've been obliged to sit in smoke-filled back rooms with pokerfaced executives. Derision, I learned, very often masks alarm.

Every seat in the courtroom is occupied. The Fan Club even camped outside the night before so they might pack the courtroom with the kind of good energy needed by a person wearing a silly bright pink suit.

Yet good energy only gets a defendant like me so far. There is still a case to argue. The State District Attorney assigned a prosecutor named Bella Blue to the case. This is a bummer on many levels, not the least of which is that Bella and I go way back. When we were both juniors in high school, Bella and I dated the same guy, some dude whose name I've forgotten. In fact, I started seeing him very soon after they'd broken up. Very, very soon, like ten minutes. All three of us had been at the same party. He kissed me, broke up with Bella, and then he and I went home together. One might say that I stole her boyfriend, except you can't actually steal a person from another person. When you're in high school, though, such fine points hardly matter.

Obviously, we aren't in high school anymore and I just have to trust that Bella has long ago moved on from the boyfriend incident. A couple of years ago we ran into one another at a conference on the state's prison system and we ended up in the hotel lobby bar having a tipsy conversation about the old days. We buried the hatchet, laughed at our younger selves, and resolved to get together for lunch, which we never did. I heard through the old high school grapevine a few months later that Bella hadn't voted for me and wasn't shy about sharing that information.

I wish now I was ignorant of her voting record. I'm okay with a person who doesn't like me. The first lesson you learn as a politician is that you can't please everyone.

It's the people who *seem* to like me but whom I suspect actually don't. They make me feel as though the earth below my feet is about ready to toss and shake.

As for the mystery of Bella's opinion on the state of my integrity, post-high school, I don't have long to wait. Her opening remarks to the jury confirm that, yes indeed, the ground on which I stand is a frying pan and it's heating up fast.

"The prosecution will prove beyond a reasonable doubt that with forethought and full intention, the defendant flaunted the electoral process, stole proprietary information, and subverted democracy in order to win an election and further her career in politics," Bella begins.

"She orchestrated a sophisticated computer hack, downloaded private corporate memos, and endangered the safety of a minor. Moreover, the State will show that the information gleaned illegally from these memos had a direct and inarguable impact on the outcome of the election. This meddling constitutes a manipulation of democracy and a profound breach of trust, perpetrated by a representative elected in good faith by the people."

Besides the fact that "sophisticated" is the last word I'd choose to describe the hack I perpetrated, the rest of Bella's accusations were sickeningly true. I sit there like a clown in my hot pink pantsuit, absorbing the reality that dispassionately described my crimes as really bad, even to me.

As she speaks, the courtroom is silent. A faint yet distinct hissing sound coming from the audience seems to bounce around the gallery, as though refusing to attach itself to any single member of the audience. As Bella speaks, I realize the hiss is a kind of collective expression of disgust from the Fan Club. The ladies in their gray hair and sensible shoes are taking turns expressing their displeasure, so subtle that, at first, I think it's some kind of accident - someone brought a balloon into the courtroom and now it's suffering a slow and uneven leak. The court clerk squints out at the crowd, catching on that some sort of mild civil disobedience is happening. As of yet, the judge hasn't reacted. Surely, she too is hearing soft, ladylike hisses rising from the benches behind me.

The moment I arrived in the courtroom and took my place next to Ophelia at the defendant's table, I looked around for Tim but didn't find him. Perhaps, having come in late, he's here now. Maybe a Fan Club member saved him a seat. More likely he isn't in the room. Tim's not the kind of person who thinks ahead. Probably he arrived this morning, discovered the courtroom full, felt lousy for his bad planning, and went home.

That I am giving Tim the benefit of the doubt feels less like a moment of denial and more like an emotional necessity. I need him to be here, if not in reality at least in spirit. I need to believe he tried.

My family, however, is making no secret of their presence. They're lined up behind me like a row of sentries, with my father in the middle, his arms crossed across his chest and a frown plastered on his face in a display of disgust for the whole sad proceeding. My mother is at his side, her spiral stenographer's notebook at the ready. As Bella speaks, I can hear my mother's pencil digging furiously into the page.

Jennifer is thumbing her cell phone, intently live-tweeting the trial. My sister and brother have chosen seats on the other side of the courtroom, directly behind the prosecutor and her supporting attorneys, in a sweet gesture that I guess is meant to intimidate the opposing legal team and/or to eavesdrop on their strategy. Tina, in her soccer mom cardigan and Billy, with his sweaty, chemo-soaked face, hardly make an imposing pair. Still, I am so moved by the determined looks on their faces that I nearly lose it.

In contrast to the harsh and frightening reality laid out by Bella's speech, Ophelia's opening argument begins like a balm on my chafed and panicked soul. Watching the jury as she speaks, I am certain they are accepting her argument as the truth. The one and only truth, so help me God.

She is good, my Ophelia. She is sharp. Earlier, she told me in the excited tones of a legal geek the jury selection process for my trial had been the most challenging of her career and that she planned to use it as a hypothetical in her course on trial law. Sadly, finding jurists in Greenville who were ignorant of the details of the election wasn't the problem—like everywhere else in America, the number of disconnected, nonvoting citizens of Greenville is depressingly high. The problem was finding people with little to no opinion on politics. One would think that a highly apathetic electorate would correspond to a dearth of strong opinion either way yet, as it turns out, there's little connection between the political vociferousness of any given Greenvillian and the tendency of said constituents to actually get off their butts and exercise their right to vote. As a constitutional law specialist, Ophelia is fascinated by this dynamic.

She claimed she was satisfied with the jury. Looking them over now, I wonder what the pool of candidates must have been like if these were the cream of the crop. I search in vain for a glimmer of intelligence in somebody's eyes. In order to qualify for the job, each jurist needed to be the kind of person who is disengaged from civic participation on even the most basic level and, moreover, who rarely reads the newspaper. Twelve people who fit this description were to decide my future.

"Ladies and Gentlemen of the jury," Ophelia begins, "the defense has no intention of arguing that the computer breach at Regional Oil didn't happen. It did. Nor will we argue that the breach didn't come from a computer at the Glass campaign. It did."

She pauses to let this information sink in. As she explained to me earlier, she learned in pre-trial discovery that the prosecution's evidence of our hack into their system was so close to irrefutable that trying to discredit it would only make us look desperate.

"However," she continues, "what the defense *will* show is the councilmember bears no responsibility for this crime. She knew nothing about the incident whatsoever and learned about it only from a member of the media who was calling for her statement. The councilmember was misled by her campaign manager, an individual who acted independently and illegally in the pursuit of her own agenda and who lied and concealed the facts. This individual has disappeared entirely. It is this individual who bears responsibility for this act, this individual who recruited the young hacker, and this individual who also has a history of inappropriate behavior with him. Given these conditions, the defense will show that the councilmember should be absolved of responsibility in this matter and receive a full exoneration by the court."

My spirits lift as Ophelia speaks. She is so convincing. She's collected, smart, and believable. I'm here in my bright pink suit, looking defiant and righteous. Surely, they will let me off. Except for the small matter of all the lies packed into Ophelia's opening statement so far, everything is going great.

The last time we spoke, I asked Ophelia how she planned to handle the political side of the equation, how she'd use—or not—the big picture, namely fracking. She admitted she hadn't yet worked it out. She told me she needed to get into the courtroom. She needed to get a look at the jury.

Clearly, she'd gotten her look and deemed her audience sympathetic because now she's going for broke. I am both delighted and terrified. It was me who'd given her the green light to do this. In fact, I insisted. I told her to use the courtroom as a pulpit, to bust the fuckers any way she could, even at the cost of my case. At first she waved me off. I was her first priority, she said. It was her job to get me exonerated. She'd only go full-on political if she thought it was in my best interest.

Ophelia must have made her assessment that full-on political was, indeed, in my best interest because here she is, taking it all the way. "Moreover, ladies and gentlemen of the jury," she continues, "the defense intends to show that the prosecution has been influenced and, indeed, corrupted by an existing dynamic between Regional Oil and my client. We will show the existence of a conspiracy—a corporate vendetta against the councilmember due to her family's connections with Regional Oil and the anti-fracking activism in which they've been engaged."

Ophelia pauses to let this information sink in.

"Three generations of my client's family," she continues, "have been employed by the company. Her brother, her father, and her grandfather. These longtime Regional Oil employees have been working closely with the whistleblower who exposed the company's recent accident cover up and its poisoning of Greenville Creek. We will prove beyond a reasonable doubt that my client has been unjustly targeted for her very inconvenient questions about the connections between the state mines inspector and Regional Oil."

She makes her opening arguments for another couple of minutes but I'm not listening anymore. With these words, it's all out in the open. I've been accused of a crime that I did, in fact, commit. Yet, my accusers are criminals, too. Before this trial is over, one of us will be going down.

Chapter Eighteen

Apart from the opening arguments, the first several hours of the trial are boring as hell. The technology team at Regional Oil leads us through an impenetrable explanation of how they captured the IP address of the campaign laptop; how they knew we'd been in their system; and how they knew which documents we'd accessed. By the time the morning is over, I have learned far more than I ever care to know about modern hacking methods and the sophisticated security systems in place to stop them.

For Ophelia's cross-examination, her first goal is to show that the hack wasn't professional. She means to prove that this word isn't just a lie but an outrageous lie, meant to suggest that more was going on than just the unauthorized actions of a rogue campaign manager and the teenage kid she seduced.

In this process, she leads our own expert witness to refute point-by-point the claims of the prosecution that the hackers had any idea whatsoever what they were doing. Together with her witness, Ophelia painted a picture of July and Frankie as clumsy and amateur. "Proof's in the pudding," the guy concludes. "They got busted, and easily, too." I realize as this argument is being so skillfully made that should my case be lost, I will not only have been proven a thief but an incompetent one, too.

Ophelia grills her expert. "Would you say that the term 'sophisticated' is such a blatant misrepresentation that it might well have been an intentional lie?"

"Objection," says Bella. "Irrelevant."

"Where are you going with this?" the judge asks Ophelia.

"It goes to the validity of the accusations against my client," she replies.

"Denied," the judge says to Bella. "Go ahead," she tells Ophelia, but the tone of her voice advises caution.

"Would you say," Ophelia continues, "that to describe this obviously bungled hacking attempt as 'sophisticated' is consistent with suspicions of conspiracy?"

"Objection," says Bella again.

"Your Honor," Ophelia addresses the judge, "I intend to argue a conspiracy between Regional Oil and the office of the state mines inspector—

The judge holds up her palm. The courtroom goes quiet. The judge knows as well as anyone that the case hinges on whether she'll allow Ophelia's line of questioning. She knows, in fact, the whole dirty business depends upon this moment because, otherwise, my case is only about a little local race in the middle of America and whether a small-time politician fixed her election. If she opens the door to Regional Oil's behavior, she brings the case to another level. If the judge denies Bella's objection, we have a shot-in-hell of winning this trial.

"Counselor," the judge says to Ophelia, "How do you plan to prove the state is under the influence of Regional Oil?"

"This line of questioning intends to show the relationship between the prosecutor's office and the state mines inspector, whose failure to cite the company for safety infractions led to the accident. In order to show the degree to which Regional Oil is interested in keeping my client quiet and the degree to which the state is supporting those interests, these questions are critical."

The judge blinks, then nods. "Proceed."

A sigh of approval rises from the Fan Club.

During the lunch break, I ask Ophelia why the prosecution seems so invested in the question of the hackers' professionalism.

"Interesting, isn't it," she says. "I didn't expect they'd lean on that angle."

"What angle?" I ask.

She gives me a look. "What angle do you think?"

"Conspiracy?" I say. "Seriously?"

"Doesn't make much sense," Ophelia says.

"What, accusing me before we can accuse them?" I whisper.

"Something like that," she says, "or maybe it's a diversion. Either way, it's good. They're uncertain of their case."

After lunch, the prosecution calls Frankie to the stand. As bad as I feel about July falling on her sword for this case, I feel even worse about its impact on Frankie. July ended her career in politics, and even her life in the U.S., all for a shot at keeping me out of jail. But she's an adult and she knew the consequences.

On the other hand, Frankie, having taken the district attorney's plea deal, is safe from prosecution. Yet to use July's word, that didn't mean he will leave this experience unscathed. His parents are certainly mortified. He'll be the subject of gossip and, despite the fact that none of his activities will end up on a permanent record, he'll still bear the emotional scars of having been betrayed by the woman he loved, outed as an inept hacker, and, worse yet, dragged through a trial with the whole humiliating business on public display.

Wearing khaki trousers, an ugly knit tie, and an ill-fitting dress shirt, Frankie approaches the witness box and takes the seat. He looks like a ten-year-old boy forced to attend church. That he is here, in this situation, is one hundred percent my fault. Endangering the welfare of a minor indeed.

I am ashamed to realize that I haven't given Frankie a second thought, beyond being furious about his disloyalty. Why should Frankie be loyal anyway, especially to me? I was a stranger and he was just a kid. If he were my son or my nephew, I would sure as hell do exactly what his parents had done, which is to encourage him, in fact, to compel him, to use any means necessary to get him to take the plea.

But when Frankie opens his mouth, the voice that emerges wasn't one of a scared child. Rather, it is the voice of a defiant and disdainful young man. He slouches in the chair, refuses to make eye contact with Bella as she asks him questions, replies in monosyllables, plays with the microphone attached to the podium, keeps winking at someone in the back row of the gallery, fidgets, and generally portrays himself as a disrespectful, entitled brat.

Ophelia writes a note on the pad in front of me. *What a little shit.*

I scribble back, *good news for us?* If Frankie is deemed unreliable by the jury, perhaps their case will weaken.

Definitely, she writes. As she told me earlier, the prosecution didn't need Frankie in order to prove the hack happened. The evidence was clear. What they needed him for was to make the jury believe that I was there in the room that night. If he was a total dick, they'd hate him and it's hard to take the word of a witness that you hate. The good news about Frankie's lousy personality is that it helps me feel slightly less terrible about changing the course of his youth. He'd probably have screwed it up without me anyway.

Bella finishes milking every drop out of Frankie's confession of the hack. Now it's Ophelia's turn to cross-examine. She begins by establishing how he came to be involved in our sad little enterprise and confirms he was recruited by my campaign manager. Finally, she's getting to the bottom of Frankie's relationship with July.

"July was your babysitter, correct?" Ophelia says.

"She sat for my little sisters," Frankie mumbles.

"Your relationship with her was different," Ophelia says. "Right?"

"Whatever," Frankie says.

"Young man," says the judge, "*whatever* is not an appropriate response."

Frankie lifts his eyes in the direction of the judge but doesn't actually look at her. "Yes," he says into the microphone "it was different."

"She had sex with you, isn't that right?" Ophelia says.

For the first time since he sat down, Frankie straightens in his seat. He leans forward and puts his mouth close to the microphone. "Yes," he replies to the suddenly silent courtroom, enunciating carefully. "Yes. She had sex with me. And also, I had sex with her. You could say that we had sex together."

Someone in the gallery giggles.

"Did July offer you a deal in exchange for the hacking job?" Ophelia says.

"What kind of deal?" Frankie responds.

"A sexual deal," says Ophelia.

Frankie inhales and leans so close to the microphone I'm sure he's going to put it right in his mouth. "Yes," he says.

Yes? I think. Did he just say Yes? What?

I swivel in my chair, looking for my sister and brother. Their faces are ashen.

"Yes?" Ophelia says, and there's no mistaking the shock in her voice.

"Uh, no, no. I mean, no," Frankie says.

"Which is it, young man?" says the judge.

"What do you mean by a deal?" Frankie says. "Like, are you asking did she say, 'hey Frankie I'll give you a blow job if you do this hack?' Like, are you asking if we shook hands on it? Because no. If you've got to shake hands to make it a deal, I guess the answer is no. It was subtler than that."

Ophelia turns away from the witness box and is idly flipping her thumb against a stack of papers. "When was the last time you had sex with July?" she asks.

"I can't remember," Frankie says, without pausing.

"How long ago?" she repeats. "Last week?"

"No," Frankie replies.

"Last month?"

"No," he says.

"Anytime during the last year? The last two years?"

"No," he says.

"Let me ask you again," Ophelia continues. "Did you take sexual favors from July in exchange for this hacking job?"

"No," Frankie says.

Whispers rise from the gallery.

"That's not what you answered before," says Ophelia.

"That's not what you asked before," he says.

The judge interrupts. She asks the court recorder to read back Ophelia's initial question.

"Did July offer you a deal in exchange for the hacking job," states the stenographer.

"The answer is yes," Frankie says, "she offered. But I said no."

Later, when this whole business was over, we would all wonder whether Frankie was telling the truth. Did July really offer to sleep with him again? It didn't matter to my case either way—their past history was plenty to establish July as a predator and, therefore, unsympathetic. However, in that moment I could see that, to

Frankie, it mattered a lot. He wanted the court to know that he'd refused the sexual advances of his beautiful ex-babysitter. That's when I knew that Frankie would go home happy and his life would turn out just fine.

Maria, the phony PR volunteer and mole from Regional Oil had just taken the stand when Tim entered the courtroom. I heard the door groan open behind me—I've become hypersensitive to the sound of that door, fighting the impulse to turn around every time I hear it.

This morning, after I had already eagerly twisted in response to the groan of that door at least half a dozen times, I felt a whack on my thigh from Ophelia. She hissed at me to cut it out. I was making everyone nervous.

So when Tim came in I didn't see him right away. Slowly, I became aware of his presence, standing against the wall of the courtroom. I turned my head and there he was, watching my face and waiting for me to turn and see him. I felt a wave of calm wash over me. Whatever happens next, at least he's here.

Ophelia would later admit what happened next was the darkest moment of the trial; when the depth of the shit we were in became truly evident.

Having established in her questioning that Maria was a volunteer for my campaign, having described the tasks she worked on, having argued that Maria, in fact, had very quickly worked her way into the inner circle, Bella Blue went in for the kill. "Were you in the office the day the newspaper story was published about the computer breach?"

"Yes," replied Maria.

"What did you hear that day?" Bella asked.

"I was in the ladies' room," Maria said, "and heard the councilmember talking to July, just before she went into the executive staff meeting."

"What did she say?"

"July was advising the councilmember to remain silent. I remember it clearly. She said, "Don't confess anything. It will only put the staff at risk.""

I remembered that conversation. I remembered, too, doing what we always did, peeking under the doors to ensure nobody was inside a stall. I grabbed my pen and scrawled a note on Ophelia's pad. *Bitch must've been standing on the toilet.*

Well, she's a spy, after all, Ophelia wrote back.

I looked across the room for Tim. The expression of dismay and disappointment on his face made me want to crawl under the defendant's table and stay there for the rest of my life.

On cross-examination, the best Ophelia could do was establish the possibility that when July told me to keep quiet, she might not have been talking about the hack.

She got Maria to admit, in fact, that she hadn't heard July refer specifically to the hack. Instead, all she heard was *'don't tell them'* on the same morning the article in the Sun broke and just before we were to head into a meeting to strategize a response.

The judge allowed Ophelia to push Maria pretty far. I was surprised at the leeway she was given to convince the jury we might have been talking about anything. It was a technical victory, but any one of the jurors with a modicum of common sense or deductive reasoning would conclude Maria heard July and me talking about our guilt. We were conspiring to keep the truth from my staff. I watched the faces of the jury as Ophelia walked away from the stand, her forehead in a tired frown. They were looking at me. Their eyes had changed and their bodies had shifted. They no longer believed I might be innocent. I wondered if they ever had.

Chapter Nineteen

J. C. Vanderpelt is a very tall man. He looks uncomfortable in the witness box, as though he doesn't have enough legroom. This is probably the story of his life. I find myself thinking that J. C. Vanderpelt must always be just a little bit uncomfortable. Always too tall. I'll bet he's always on the lookout for low hanging branches, for old doorways, and for overhead bins. I wonder how many times Vanderpelt has whacked his head, just trying to negotiate a world built for short people.

It's the second day of the trial. I'm back in the hot pink pantsuit. This time Ginny has paired the suit with a tangerine camisole, a brooch handcrafted by a local artisan from a vintage suffragette lapel pin, and camel suede slingbacks with a creamy patent leather toe. Once again, I look smashing on the outside and feel disgusting on the inside.

Ophelia finished preliminary questions to Vanderpelt, establishing for the jury he'd been a loyal Regional

Oil employee, in their employ for 14 years with the last three as night crew chief at the Greenville processing plant. She spent several long minutes reading aloud excerpts from Vanderpelt's personnel file, obtained from his union representative, Shirley McRyan, both an invaluable resource for the case as well as a huge pain in the neck to Ophelia. During one of her jail visits, she told me McRyan had crawled so far up her ass about keeping her client protected from whistleblower persecution that she'd be walking funny for weeks after this thing is over.

Ophelia is reading aloud a series of excerpts she cherry-picked from Vanderpelt's employee evaluation reports over the last decade. Vanderpelt's personnel file, according to Ophelia, was one of the luckiest breaks we've had in the trial. It read like a series of fan letters, an avalanche of admiration. One supervisor after another, it was all the same: J. C. Vanderpelt was a conscientious worker, an effective leader, and an asset to the company. They all predicted a bright future for him at Regional Oil.

Ophelia removes her reading glasses and hands a piece of paper to Vanderpelt. "Would you please identify this document?" she asks.

Vanderpelt frowns at the piece of paper. He holds it awkwardly with three of his long fingers. "This is an email I sent to my supervisor on the day of the oil tank accident."

"Your supervisor at the time was Billy Glass, correct?"

Vanderpelt confirms this and Ophelia asks him to read the memo aloud.

"The well started leaking fracking fluid and spewing oil on Thursday around 08:45," Vanderpelt read. Here at last is the memo we found, the one so compelling I took the risk to download it and thereby get caught and sent to jail. Had I known it would land me here in this courtroom, would I have made that decision again?

"The spill will take a couple more days to clear up," Vanderpelt continues. "The well lost control after the blowout preventer failed. It's leaking 50 to 70 barrels per day. We're trucking the fluids away from the site. We're diverting and sandbagging as best we can but we're losing roughly sixty percent of the spill into Greenville Creek."

"Mr. Vanderpelt, can you tell the jury what happened after you sent the memo?"

"Nothing happened," he says.

"Normally what would you expect to happen?" Ophelia asks.

"Well, for starters, they'd put together a cleanup plan. Assign a crew of guys. Call a team meeting. Go over who does what."

"How long after a spill would you expect that meeting to be called?"

"When you're losing that much fluid, pretty damn quick."

"Within a few hours, let's say?"

Vanderpelt nods yes and the judge asks him to verbalize his responses.

"Yes, your Honor. And three hours later we're hearing nothing, so I asked Billy about the cleanup plan. Which guys we'd put on the team, etcetera."

"And what did he tell you?" Ophelia says.

"He told me to get back to work."

"What did you do?"

Vanderpelt hesitates and looks at the jury. "I went back to work."

"Knowing the oil and fluid was still leaking? You didn't question the decision? You didn't push Mr. Glass? You didn't protest?"

"At Regional Oil, you don't protest," Vanderpelt says. "You keep your nose to the ground and you do your job."

"Even when something has gone terribly wrong?" Ophelia says.

"Especially then," Vanderpelt says. "And it isn't like Billy Glass had any control over the situation. There's nothing he could have done either."

"But, what about the company's grievance procedures? What about your labor union?"

"All of that sounds real nice when it's printed in the
manuals," Vanderpelt replies. "Real life at Regional Oil
is something else."

"What's real life like?" Ophelia asks. "How does the
company make life difficult for employees who try to
speak truth to power?"

"Objection," Bella Blue says. "Inflammatory!"

Before the judge can say anything, Ophelia with-
draws the question. She takes a few slow steps across the
courtroom, picks up her legal pad from our table, consults her notes.

"Mr. Vanderpelt," she finally says, "did you ever know
anyone else who tried to blow the whistle at Regional
Oil?"

"There was Lucy, the girl in the field office," he says.
"The secretary who worked onsite, in the trailer."

"Lucy Jackson," says Ophelia, glancing at her notes.
"What about Lucy Jackson?"

"She got sexually harassed," Vanderpelt says.

"Objection!" Bella Blue screeches. "Your honor, this
line of questioning is utterly irrelevant. This has nothing to do with the alleged accident."

"I'm showing a pattern of employee intimidation,"
Ophelia says.

"Go ahead," says the judge, leaning forward in her chair.

"As far as you know, Mr. Vanderpelt, did Lucy Jackson file a complaint, as per the company's procedure in the employee handbook?"

"Yes, she did, for all the good that did her."

"You and Lucy Jackson were acquainted outside of work, were you not?"

"She was my kids' soccer coach," Vanderpelt says.

"Can you speak to her character?"

"She was a damn fine girl. A good coach, nice person. My sons liked her, my wife liked her. At work, she did her job, went home. No nonsense. And knowing who she was complaining about, we all believed her."

"Who was she complaining about?"

"Someone in the executive office," Vanderpelt says.

"Is that person here in the courtroom?" Ophelia asks.

"Your Honor!" Bella Blue says. "This is hearsay!"

"Approach the bench, both of you," the judge says, and the rest of us are left to strain to hear their whispering. Ophelia says something and the judge leans back in her chair, throwing Bella Blue a stern look. When they turn around, Ophelia has a tiny smug grin on her lips. She's having a very good day.

Ophelia turns to her witness and asks the question again. "Is the person named in Lucy Jackson's sexual harassment claim here in the courtroom?"

Vanderpelt raises his finger and points. All heads swivel. We all look towards the entourage and the CEO of Regional Oil. Specifically, he's pointing at the tall redhead in the tiger skin shoes.

"Please let the record show the witness has indicated Eleanor Allison, the Vice President of Public Affairs for Regional Oil," Ophelia says. "Mr. Vanderpelt, why do you say you believed Lucy Jackson when she said she was sexually harassed by Ms. Allison?"

"Well, first of all, because like my wife says, girls in the workplace don't file those kinds of complaints against their boss unless it's serious. Because they know people just won't believe them. So, when they do, they're taking a risk. They have a lot to lose. And second, because Lucy was an honest person, a straight shooter, no pun intended. And third, because everyone knows Ms. Allison is a bitch on wheels."

"Your Honor, please," Bella Blue interjects, quietly.

"Please watch your language, sir," the judge says.

"Can you tell me what happened when Lucy Jackson filed this complaint?" Ophelia asks him.

"She was threatened," he says, "she told me they said if she didn't drop the complaint they would call her parents, tell them she's a lesbian."

"Your Honor," Bella Blue says, her body language showing defeat even before she finishes speaking. "Again, hearsay."

"Forget it," says the judge. Whatever Ophelia whispered to her earlier clearly had an impact. "Continue, counselor."

"Why was Lucy so worried about her parents finding out about her sexuality?"

"They were bible thumpers," Vanderpelt says. "When Lucy was a teenager, they sent her to one of those cult camps, the ones that supposedly make you not gay anymore. It really messed with her head. Sometimes Lucy used to come over after the games, to barbeques at our place. Once she talked to me and my wife about her past. Her father was pretty abusive. Lucy found it easier—less traumatic—to let him believe she was straight, that the camp had worked."

"Mr. Vanderpelt, I'm sure the members of jury are asking themselves why the defense doesn't simply call Lucy Jackson to the stand, rather than asking you—a coworker and friend—to tell us her story. Can you tell us why?"

Across the courtroom, all four of the locker room women from Regional Oil are glaring stone-faced at Vanderpelt.

"Because Lucy is dead," Vanderpelt said. "A week after they threatened her, Lucy killed herself."

And here my brilliant Ophelia goes in for the kill. "Why did you finally decide to blow the whistle, Mr.

Vanderpelt?" she asks. "Why, after all these months, did you at last decide to come forward and tell the truth?"

"They're bad people, ma'am. They don't care about Greenville, they don't care about workers, or about accidents, or about the oil in the creek. They don't care they put a man in a wheelchair that day. But I'm ashamed to say those aren't my reasons. I'm doing this because my boys lost a good soccer coach, a good role model. Again he points and all heads swivel to two little blonde kids, looking intimidated by the attention. They're sitting with their mother, who has tears streaming down her face and a look of pride in her husband that just about kills me.

"It's not right what they did to Lucy," Vanderpelt says. "She's why I'm here. I'm doing this for her. I'm doing this to show my boys how to do the right thing."

Bella Blue's cross-examination of J. C. Vanderpelt focuses on one strategy — to discredit our next witness, my brother Billy. She approaches the stand and plants her feet.

"Mr. Vanderpelt," she says, in a voice that is too loud, as though she were speaking to the guard posted at the doorway on the other side of the room. "I'd like to ask about your supervisor, Billy Glass. You testified that he told you to get back to work the day of the storage tank accident. Later, he had second thoughts about his actions that day, is that right?"

"We all had second—"

"So the answer is yes? He did question himself, later on? He changed his mind?"

"Objection, your honor," Ophelia says.

"Denied," says the judge. "Go ahead, counselor."

"Did Mr. Glass have a change of heart?" she asks.

"I don't know," replies Vanderpelt. "I'm not inside his heart."

A guy in the jury snickers.

"Let me rephrase," Bella Blue says. "Seven months after the accident, did Mr. Glass come to you and ask you to corroborate his story?"

"Yes," Vanderpelt says. "But it wasn't *his* story. It was—"

"Did he pressure you, Mr. Vanderpelt? Did he threaten you in any way?"

"Absolutely not, no, there were no threats."

"But pressure? There was pressure, wasn't there? He ordered you, didn't he? He ordered you to blow the whistle?"

"This is my decision," Vanderpelt says, "entirely."

"But this whole thing was his idea, wasn't it? Isn't he the instigator here? Didn't he take you to lunch just a few weeks ago, just before the election? Didn't he ask you then to testify?"

"Yes, but I was already considering—"

"It wasn't until his sister was running for city council, indeed it wasn't until her campaign was in trouble, that Billy Glass invited you to lunch, isn't that true?"

"He didn't pressure me," Vanderpelt says calmly.

"Did Billy Glass tell you why you should corroborate his story?"

"He didn't need to tell me. I'm doing it because—"

Beside me, Ophelia picks up her pen. *Crap,* she wrote on the yellow pad.

Do something! I scribble back.

Like what?? she writes, and slams the pen onto the desk.

She is right to be angry. If there were any chance Billy might have coerced Vanderpelt, she should have been warned.

"Answer the question, Mr. Vanderpelt," Bella Blue says. "Did Mr. Glass give you a reason why you should come forward with these accusations?"

"He has cancer," Vanderpelt says. "He didn't exactly need to explain why—"

"Mr. Vanderpelt, please answer the question. Did Billy Glass tell you why he wanted you to cooperate?"

"Yes," Vanderpelt says.

"What did he say?"

Vanderpelt looks at the judge. "Your honor," he protests.

"Sorry, sir, you'll need to answer the question," she tells him.

Vanderpelt looks at Billy, still sitting behind the prosecutor's table, and I can see the misery in his eyes. "He told me he needed to get his sister elected. He said I should come forward because if I didn't she would lose."

Bella Blue turns her back on Vanderpelt. "No more questions, your Honor."

"But wait," Vanderpelt says. "Wait, I have more to say! I agreed with him, I think it's crucial—"

"No more questions!" Bella Blue shouts and, although J. C. Vanderpelt tries to keep talking, the judge tells him to be quiet. She thanks him for his testimony and tells him to step down. When he passes my table, he reaches out his hand and with those long awkward fingers he squeezes my shoulder.

Chapter Twenty

The court recesses for lunch. When I stand from the defense table, a wave of nausea overtakes me and I need to sit again. My last chemo treatment was a few days ago and the misery has mostly subsided. But this stress is not helping. Neither is the bright orange and electric pink of my outfit. All I want is to crawl into my prison sweat suit, curl up on my bunk, and listen to Mercedes tell stories about her family.

We eat our sandwiches—or rather Ophelia eats hers and I stare at mine in disgust—on a metal table in a dingy little meeting cubicle next to the courtroom. "Listen," Ophelia says. "I haven't changed my mind. I think you shouldn't testify."

In the beginning, back when I'd first been taken into custody and Ophelia and I began discussing our strategy, I insisted that above anything, I needed to testify. Ophelia said I shouldn't, that it wouldn't help and might do more harm than good. I fought her on this long and hard.

Naturally, I wanted to tell my story. I wanted my moment in the witness box. When you're a politician, it looks terrible not to testify; it looks like you're afraid of something, namely the truth. I couldn't bear the idea of being seen as a liar and I told her so.

I pick up my sandwich, examine the ham and cheese, and put it down again. Ophelia continues. "You're just going to need to deal with the reality that some people will always, for the rest of your life, believe you're guilty. Taking the stand in an attempt to convince the inconvincible is a stupid decision that could likely land you in prison. Please, Peg. Please just shut up and let me do the talking."

My body hurts all over. Beneath this jaunty and cheerful pink suit, I'm a mess. Ophelia is right. I have practically no fight left in me. I'm not afraid of a debate, especially a public one. I've been grilled by the press and by the mayor and by angry constituents. Six months ago, a courtroom testimony would have been a piece of cake. I'd have wiped the floor with Bella Blue, never mind the whole high school boyfriend thing. But today? Well, today I'm different. Not to mention the irritating fact that Bella Blue is well-rested and she doesn't have cancer.

Besides, the fewer times I have to lie about my innocence the better. "Okay," I tell my lawyer, my friend. "You win. I won't testify."

She takes my hand. "You don't look so great, Peg," she says. "Come on, you need to lie down. There's a couch in the lawyers' lounge. It's off limits, but tough shit."

Ophelia leads me down the hall, taking me to the lounge and leaving me there on the couch. For the next twenty minutes, she stands outside the door, sending everyone away.

After the lunch break, Ophelia calls my brother Billy to the stand. Her strategy from this point forward in the trial is to lean hard on the conspiracy angle, building a case that leads to the state mines inspector.

"Mr. Glass," Ophelia begins, "were you on duty at Regional Oil the day of the storage tank accident?" When Billy replies yes, she goes on to establish his position at the company, his job responsibilities, and the long relationship between Regional Oil and the Glass Family. "The company has employed a total of twelve members of your extended family, isn't that true, Mr. Glass?"

"I have a lot of cousins," Billy says, turning on the charm. At least four members of the jury smile in recognition.

"Mr. Glass, kindly describe for the jury the standard operating procedure for reporting an accident at the plant."

"I fill out a form 344F," Billy replies. "Then I send it to my supervisor."

"Baxter Sherman," Ophelia says.

"Right."

"What happened when you sent your report to Mr. Sherman?"

"I didn't send the report," Billy says.

"Why is that, Mr. Glass?"

"Because I didn't write one. Baxter told me not to. He said he'd take care of it."

"To your knowledge, did he do that? Did he file the report himself?"

"To my knowledge, no."

"If he had filed the report, to whom would he have sent it?"

"To the office of the state mines inspector," Billy replies.

"Really?" Ophelia says. "He doesn't send the report to his boss?"

"At Baxter's management level, he's required to report any accident straight to the state. The executive office is copied, of course."

"Your honor," says Ophelia, "let me enter into evidence the accident roster from the office of the state mines inspector for the period in question. You'll note that no report was received during that month from Regional Oil."

She turns to Billy and asks, "Is this kind of thing unusual? Has this happened before, to your knowledge? A supervisor ordering a worker to squelch information?"

"Objection!" cries Bella Blue, "inflammatory!"

"Your honor," says Ophelia, "if telling an employee not to file a report on an industrial accident that resulted in an active and ongoing leak of—" she consults her notes—"300 gallons of fracking fluid per hour into Greenville Creek is not in fact the definition of squelching information, I'm not sure what is."

"You may answer the question, Mr. Glass," the judge says.

"I have no direct knowledge of this kind of thing happening before," Billy says, "but after this experience, I wouldn't be surprised if this wasn't the first time."

"Objection," says Bella Blue, "speculative."

The judge nods her head in agreement and orders the stenographer to erase Billy's comment from the record. She asks the jury to disregard what he just said. "Please stick to answering the questions, Mr. Glass," she tells Billy.

"I understand you are suffering from leukemia," Ophelia says, "and that you personally believe your cancer is workplace related."

"Damn right," says Billy.

"You haven't exactly been quiet about this theory, have you? In fact, you might say you've become something of an activist, is that accurate? An anti-fracking activist?"

"Correct," he says.

"Must make things tough at work," Ophelia says. "You're probably not too popular around the drill site."

"My men and I get along just fine," Billy says. "It's management that's the problem."

"Did you receive your diagnosis of cancer and begin treatment before or after the fuel tank explosion?"

"Before. I'd known for a couple of weeks."

"Did you tell anyone at work?"

"One or two people," he says. "Apparently word got out, pretty quickly, though."

I was hit by a pang of guilt. How had I not known he had cancer? All of Billy's coworkers knew, but not me. Was I really that out of touch with my family?

"Is it fair to say that by the time of the fuel tank explosion, most of your co-workers were aware of your diagnosis?"

"That would be fair, yes," he replies.

"Would you say that management was also in the loop regarding your health status?"

"Damn right," Billy responds, at the very same moment that Bella Blue rises halfway up from her chair to lodge an objection. "Your honor," she continues, raising her voice over Billy's. "Relevance!"

"Fine, I'll rephrase," Ophelia says. "Do you have reason to believe that management saw you as a liability?"

"They've been trying to fire me ever since I got leukemia," Billy says.

"Because you're seen as a troublemaker, isn't that right? Tell me, what did you do after you were ordered to cover up the storage tank accident? Anything at all?"

"Not at first," Billy says, "but then I started getting sick from the cancer treatments. And a few months later, my sister gets cancer and, I don't know, I just realized I couldn't do it anymore. I couldn't keep going to work at that place like everything was normal."

"So, what did you do?" Ophelia asks.

Billy's face is plastered with the same mischievous grin he's carried around all his life - the grin he uses to charm just about everyone. He leans forward to speak clearly into the microphone. "I told my mom," he says.

The judge bangs her gavel to get the people in the courtroom to quit laughing. Members of the jury are covering their mouths but their eyes reveal their delight. All his life, everybody has loved Billy. Strange that I've turned out to be the politician, considering Billy is the one born with all the natural charm.

"What happened after you told your mom?" Ophelia says.

"Well, the family got serious then, I suppose," Billy says. "You could say we started a little bit of a crusade. We got political."

"You and the family started making noise," she says. "And your father and grandfather, too; both retired from Regional Oil. Let me ask you this, Mr. Glass. Do you think the Glass family's outspokenness has anything to do with why your sister finds herself in this courtroom today?"

"Really?" standing, Bella Blue says, "Your Honor, honestly. Relevance!"

"Counselor, where are you going with this?" asks the judge.

"Showing that Regional Oil has a vendetta against the defendant because of her family's perceived disloyalty to the company and that this formed the basis for the conspiracy that included officers at Regional Oil, the state mines inspector, the campaign of the defendant's political opponent, the Greenville Republican Party, and finally the office of Senator McCray."

"Objection sustained," the judge says. "Let's stick to the case before us, counselor."

"No more questions, your honor," Ophelia says.

As she turns her back to the stand, her face is unreadable but I know she's feeling good. Her question to Billy wasn't allowed by the judge but his response wasn't the point. The point was the question itself. Ophelia sits and below the table she gives my knee a firm little pat of satisfaction.

Bella Blue's redirect of Billy is brutal and takes forever. She spends an hour discrediting him. She is relentless. She has done her homework.

Years ago after a rough patch in his marriage, Billy showed up drunk at work and ran a forklift into a ditch. Another time he had an argument with a coworker that came to blows. Fourteen years on the job, conflicts happen and especially with tough guys like these teamsters. But this is all Bella has in order to make Billy look unreliable. So she digs and pokes and makes him bleed. The spectacle of my brother being beat up like this is terrible. I can feel my body going weaker, my face going more pale, my heartbeat quickening, and the sweat forming on my brow.

Billy, too, looks awful. His chemo treatments make mine look like a Sunday sail on calm Lake Greenville. I don't know how he's enduring it. His face is ghost white and he seems to be very cold.

Bella Blue, however, doesn't seem to notice. She keeps grilling him. She's got reports from his employee file in her hand, shaking them at him, making him read aloud an unfavorable employee evaluation from eight years earlier. Billy looks like he's about to faint.

The jury is noticing this. Given the appalled looks on the faces of at least three jurors, they're seeing that the prosecuting attorney is being a real bitch to the guy with leukemia. And that the guy with leukemia is putting on a very brave front, pretending he's all right. Bella Blue seems to have entered some kind of litigation zone. She's so wrapped up in her prosecutorial zeal that she's become blind to the person she's grilling.

Finally, the judge puts us out of our misery. She holds up her hand. "Mr. Glass, would you like to take a break?"

This seems to snap Bella Blue out of her lawyerly fog. I watch her face as it dawns on her what she's just done; she's made her witness more sympathetic to my defense. "Yes!" she exclaims, trying to recover but looking desperate, like a person who's just realized how badly she's screwed up. "Please, Mr. Glass—" she begins.

But she's too late. Billy vomits. All over the witness stand. All over the microphone. The vomit splatters widely, a long stream of it landing on Bella Blue's skirt and dripping down her legs to settle on her shoes. Inside her shoes, in fact.

"Court is recessed," the judge says, banging her gavel. In that instant, Billy's eyes find mine. As our eyes connect, his mouth lifts into a grin, a private grin just for me. I nearly shout with laughter. My brother. My darling little brother.

Chapter Twenty-One

I didn't see Tim again until four days after the trial. After I was found guilty, Ophelia argued on humanitarian grounds that because I was recovering from chemotherapy, I should be allowed to await my sentencing hearing from the comfort of my home. I was more than halfway expecting Tim to be here to welcome me when I got home. But when I opened my front door, I found only a pile of mail on the floor in the hallway. My sister settled me in, made me soup, and then left.

At last. It has been so long since I'd been alone.

To hear the verdict—*guilty*—uttered aloud in the courtroom was the shock of my life. I had really, really convinced myself I'd be found not guilty.

It's amazing, now, to look back at the person I was four days ago. I was a person who believed she'd gotten away with it. I was a person who thought she could commit election fraud and not be punished. It's hard to believe.

Then again, as Ophelia argued in her closing statements, my actions were for a righteous cause. My intentions were pure.

Tim didn't call the day after my release, nor the day after and, now, it's been four days. I stand here at the kitchen sink, worrying about what's to become of us and whether I made a terrible mistake allowing myself to hope I was getting back together with my ex-husband.

My phone rings. It's him. I've conjured him up, I think. And then I remind myself I've been conjuring him for four days now. A man calls when a man calls, and not a moment sooner.

"Finally," I start.

"Yes, sorry," he says. "I was—"

"I forgive you," I say.

He exhales a chuckle. "You're a tough one."

"I don't care why you didn't call, frankly," I tell him, although of course that's not true. I care deeply, and I'm afraid to ask why he didn't call because I think I know the answer. "I'm just glad you did."

"Can I come over?" he asks.

Beyond a couple of jailhouse hugs, we haven't touched one another since that afternoon in the woods after the O'Connor fundraiser. I spent too many hours in that lousy cell thinking about this moment. Thinking about this moment got me through those low points in the courtroom.

When Tim arrives, he is carrying wine, pasta Bolognese, ice cream and a bouquet of tulips.

At the taste of his mouth, I nearly lose my balance. I kiss him in the hallway before he has a chance to take off his coat or put down his packages. His lips on mine now are like the delivery of a promise.

He pulls away and brushes past me to my kitchen table. *Our* kitchen table. "How about I put this stuff down," he says.

I'm still living in the house we bought together more than fifteen years ago. This is the table where we ate roughly four thousand dinners together. I stand in the doorway and watch him locate the corkscrew and start a pot of water for the pasta, reaching for the olive oil and the salt and the wine glasses and finding them in the same places they've always been.

He hands me a glass of Bordeaux. "Thank you for being at the trial," I say.

He raises his glass to mine. "Here's to the minimum sentence," he replies.

"Ouch," I say.

"Sorry, darling," he replies, and I rest my forehead against his chest and accept a proper embrace. In his arms I've finally come home. If only I could stay. I feel like I've been to purgatory and now I'm back for a quick spaghetti dinner before my departure to hell.

"What the fuck have I done," I say into his shirt.

"You broke the law, looks like," he tells me.

Irritated, I pull away, "What's with you? Why the hostility?"

When he places his wine glass on the table and crosses his arms over his chest, I realize once again I've missed the cues. He's pissed.

Well, I'm pissed, too.

"Why didn't you call me?" I ask. I sound like a petulant teenager. "Don't answer that," I continue. "I don't care why you didn't call me."

"Why didn't you tell me you were guilty, Peg?"

"We both know I'm not guilty," I sputter. "Not in the moral sense, not how it matters."

"You made your choice," he says.

"I put my neck on the line."

"And now you're paying for it."

"Exactly, yes! Do you think I need you to point this out to me? What's your problem, Tim?"

"You still think you're the only one who suffers from your actions."

And here we are. Back to the essential problem of our marriage, according to Tim. I'm selfish, and he's my enabler. Therefore, his job is to point out my flaws. Otherwise he's condoning my behavior. All of this is according to a mediocre couples' therapist named Allen, whom we saw for three sessions about a thousand years ago. I hated Allen and Tim loved him.

This is what you get when you end a relationship suddenly. The old baggage comes back and when you open it, everything inside is still there, only now it's dank and mildewed.

I pull the dinner plates from the cupboard and the placemats from the drawer and place them on the table. "Evidently you've been thinking things over," I say.

"I can't believe you stole that data, Peg." He's leaning against the counter, a wooden spoon in his hand, waiting for the water to boil.

"I mean, you actually did it, didn't you? When that woman from Regional Oil was on the stand testifying about their relationship with the mines commission, I was thinking, 'oh my god, Peg really did it'. The mines commission! The senate seat! You're really that ruthless? I mean, Peg, everyone knows you're ambitious but you'd really go this far? You'd commit fraud to keep the Senate seat open?"

"This has nothing to do with me!" I protest. "This isn't like before—"

"Oh, it isn't?" he interrupts.

"I have no interest in the Senate, Tim. I made that clear at least seven years ago."

I'd had a shot at the race and turned it down. The local party leadership approached me early on, before the incumbent announced his retirement. I told them no thanks. The Senate is a thankless job and no place for a bulldog like me. I'm bored by the idea of negotiating with fascists and I can't stand wearing bright colors. I told them—and myself—that the difference I can make to Greenville here at the local level was probably more lasting. Besides, my marriage was crumbling and I was having an affair. So, it didn't seem the right time to put myself in the public eye.

"Seven years? Things change," Tim says. "Opinions change, ideas change. But your ambition? You've always been ambitious and you always will be. I don't believe for a second that you didn't have your eye on the Senate. You thought you'd just expose Regional Oil and their relationship with your opponent and the Mines Commissioner and the Republicans and then you'd slip into the Senate on a landslide vote like the hero who toppled the corporate oligarchy." He slid the spaghetti from its wrapper and aggressively snapped a handful in half, sending bits skittering across the stove and dumping it into the pot.

"Nice speech," I say.

Last week in the courtroom, Sheila Maguire had her speech prepared, too. Once she started speaking from the witness box you could tell that she'd been working with a professional. The effect was as though she'd seen an old fashioned elocution coach. Each word measured, her delivery was precise and careful. Although this made her look strangely plastic, it also bestowed her with a sense of authority and confidence.

Sheila Maguire was both corporate titan and Stepford wife. When she started speaking about the rights of a private company to its proprietary information, the betrayal of their shareholders by an elected official, the increasing encroachment of government surveillance and the entitled attitude of public servants, well, she sounded credible.

Ophelia's cross examination did us no good. She had a two-pronged strategy to expose Regional Oil's history of good-old-boy backroom dealings with the state mines commission—the first prong being evidence of their failure to inspect the faulty storage tank and the second being the history of corporate donations to the independent campaign committees running negative ads against his opponent. Ultimately, the judge threw out the whole political conspiracy angle on the grounds that it wasn't relevant to the charges against me.

When she said the conspiracy wasn't relevant, I leapt to my feet. I'd had enough. I was wired and nauseous and sweating through the pink suit jacket. I couldn't handle it any more. I couldn't handle being silent, being quiet, not even having a single moment to defend myself. I suppose I went a little bit crazy from the feeling of being gagged. I stood, leaning on the table, and I yelled.

"No," I clamored. "No, no, oh come on! Your honor, this can't be! This is the whole crux of the matter! This is how they get away with it!"

Vaguely I heard a voice—was it the judge or was it the court clerk? — insisting on my silence. I ignored it and kept talking, kept on speaking, making noise.

"The spill, the toxins in the creek, the sick children, the heavy metals, the poisoning of Greenville! It comes down to this, to buying the mines commissioner—." Now I felt Ophelia's hand on my arm, pulling me down, her voice insistent, but I kept talking anyway, now yelling I suppose "—to buying the Senate, to making people sick, to working them into the ground, to ruining families and killing chickens and giving leukemia to people's brothers—and you wonder why I took the memos, you wonder why I went looking for proof of their evil, those immoral fucks, they don't give a rat's ass—"

Finally, the world came reeling back into focus and I saw myself as I was: a ranting, sweaty madwoman, hair stuck to my lipstick and ankle wobbling, confessing her crime to a stunned jury, leaning on the table for support and running out of words, running out of steam.

I sat down heavily in my chair and put my face in my hands. By the time the verdict came back guilty, nobody including me was surprised.

Tim has turned his back to me and is furiously stirring the pasta.

"Why are you yelling at me?" I ask him softly.

He lay the wooden spoon on the counter and turns to face me.

"Just when I have you back," he says. He stands there in that warrior pose I recognize, ready for an argument.

"I know," I say to him.

"Prison, Peg," he says.

"I know. But listen."

"Listen? Listen to what? You're going to fucking prison."

I get up from my seat and go to him. I wrap my arms around his neck and wipe the tears that appear without notice. I kiss his wet cheeks, his clenched hands, and his tense neck. I unbutton his shirt and unbuckle his pants.

We get naked on the kitchen floor, just like old times. The pasta boils. The wine breathes.

Chapter Twenty-Two

The morning of the Boland Run for Cancer Research dawns bright and clear. I am wide awake, watching the sunrise. Tim and I were up all night, making love and arguing and crying and laughing and then making love again. He's finally exhausted now, fast asleep diagonally across the bed, just like old times. I stand at the window and watch the sky change color. Over the treetops at the end of my street, beyond the row of television vans parked outside my house, the clouds turn from soothing blues and whites to hostile, burning pink.

Behind me in the closet hangs the famous pink suit. My feelings about the suit have evolved. This has been helped by the fact that my staff was right: the damn thing was made for the media. Newspapers and TV outlets did exactly as we hoped. They seized upon the suit as a symbol of my case. Over the course of the trial my story evolved beyond that of a righteously law-breaking local city council member into an epic tale of a woman who risks it all to expose the vile relationship between fracking, cancer, politics, and corporate corruption.

Thanks in large part to that pink suit, my story went viral. In the ten days since my conviction I have spoken with journalists from Los Angeles to Lhasa Apso. I lost count at somewhere around 25 interviews. Rachel Maddow devoted an entire twelve minutes to the story.

I wear the suit in every interview, with Ginny keeping me tastefully yet boldly accessorized. Last week, Jimmy Fallon worked Ginny's creativity into his opening routine, assembling a gently mocking montage of the diversity of necklaces, scarves and hair accessories I've sported for the cameras.

Last week I remarked over this as Jennifer—who, by the way, has changed her major to political science—was fussing over the bright enamelware brooch on my lapel just before my umpteenth interview. The clasp was bent and the thing kept hanging crookedly.

"Once again," I complained, when the cameras stopped rolling as she went looking for a safety pin, "a woman's credibility hinges upon her outfit."

Jennifer stopped rooting through my kitchen junk drawer. She ignored the crew of sneakered men and high-heeled women crowding my house and invading the last corner of my privacy. "Get over yourself, Aunt Peg," she cried out, "the suit is no longer a suit. It's a protest sign. Suck it up and smile big because you're totally rocking the visuals."

The media love to interview people living under house arrest, especially those as I am who await sentencing. The media have been scrambling to get their interviews before I'm put in the slammer. To the joy of my mother, Diane Sawyer came to visit. She sat calmly on my couch as my mother watched from the kitchen door, trembling with excitement. Every single cameramen that came stomping through my living room aimed his lens at my ankle bracelet, which kept slipping out from beneath my pink pant leg.

Initially the house arrest meant I couldn't attend the Boland Walk. This came as a huge relief. The Fan Club, however, was bitterly disappointed. Apparently they'd planned some sort of elaborate street theater protest in response to having learned that Regional Oil would re-launch their pink drill bit campaign at the rally before the Boland Run. Now that I've lost and they've won, I guess they're ready to unsheathe their pink phalluses for all the world to see.

In any case, I was delighted that I couldn't be there. As a convicted criminal, I had no desire to parade myself through the streets of Greenville. But my staff and my lawyer put their heads together and petitioned for my sentencing hearing to be extended two days. Unfortunately, I could appear at the Boland

Run after all. I am due in court two hours after the event begins.

The starting line is at the Greenville Mall on Route One. The route will wind through the new chain store commercial district and then into the funkier, older commercial streets with their locally-owned cafes and independent shops. We will walk through the university campus and beyond that to the grander, leafier neighborhoods and eventually to downtown Greenville, finishing at the public plaza by City Hall just across the street from the courthouse.

I'll simply be using the same route to get to the hearing. My staff informed me about this plan after they already arranged it, as though I may as well get used to the feeling of having no choice over my comings and goings.

Behind me, Tim stirs. "Come to bed," he murmurs. So, I do.

I spoon up next to my supposedly estranged husband and close my eyes. He drapes a heavy arm around my waist. I won't fall asleep, which is okay. I don't want to sleep. I want to soak up this feeling, the feeling of comfort and love. I want to fill my spare tank with it. For the next eighteen to twenty-two months, I will need these emergency reserves.

"Twenty-two months!" my mother wailed. This was last Sunday. We were in my kitchen, up to our elbows in meal preparation. My house arrest made it necessary to move the Glass Family Sunday Dinner to my house. I spooned the mashed potatoes into a serving dish. My mother finished making the gravy and Billy opened the wine. Jennifer stood at her grandmother's side, handing her ingredients and implements as instructed. For the last twenty minutes my mother had been periodically muttering the length of my prison sentence under her breath. We'd been ignoring her but now her whispers and murmurs were becoming cries.

"Twenty-two!" she said again.

"Eighteen with good behavior," Jennifer reminded her quietly.

"Just don't go shanking anyone, sis," said Billy, pulling a bottle of pinot noir from the wine rack. "We'll see you in a year and a half, no sweat."

He bumped my mother's hip to shift her away from the utensil drawer and began rooting around for a corkscrew. The dismal reality settled over me like a cloud of toxic dust. By the time I got out of prison, Billy was unlikely to be alive.

I stood at the counter over a steaming bowl of organic broccoli and realized these vegetables certainly weren't grown anywhere near Greenville, given that organic farming with poisoned water makes for a hard row to hoe.

The price I paid for my transgressions is not the irreversible damage to my political career, nor is it the humiliation of incarceration, nor is it even a blow to justice. The price I'm paying—the worst outcome to this whole debacle—is that I will miss the last year of my brother's life and, when the time comes, I won't be able to give him a proper goodbye.

I sliced an overly generous pat of butter from the stick and dropped it onto the broccoli. What's the point of trying to eat healthy, I thought, recklessly adding even more butter to the vegetables and more salt while I was at it. You eat. You work. You die. If you're lucky, you don't go to jail along the way.

I felt my mother's hand on my shoulder and realized I'd been crying into the broccoli. "Oh, honey," she said.

Then they surrounded me in a Glass Family group hug, Billy and Tina and Jennifer and my mother, with everyone making little *awww* sounds as if I were the one who needed comfort. My father walked into the room and, without so much as a hitch in his step, joined our huddle. He rested there for a moment, his long arms encompassing all five of us. We all breathed for a bit, together, sharing our grief and exhaustion. I had a sense of weightlessness, as though it was no longer my own legs holding me up but the legs of my loved ones.

Finally, my father cleared his throat and spoke, maintaining his grip on the family and holding the group together as he's always done.

He pulled us in harder, squeezing the circle uncomfortably tight.

"Ow," said Jennifer amiably.

"Listen, everyone," he said. "I have an important question for you."

He paused dramatically and nobody inhaled or exhaled. He was waiting for someone to take the bait.

"What, Dad?" I finally asked. "What's the question?"

"Why the hell are we hugging?"

Naturally we Glass folk found this hilarious and the huddle broke up into desperately uncontrolled group laughter. We reached for the countertops and the barstools and the appliances, each of us holding on, gasping for air inside his or her own solitary hell of pain and joy. It was the kind of moment that makes you feel simultaneously loved and desperate.

Eventually I climb out of my sleeping Tim's arms and into the shower. I'm due at the courthouse at noon. The Boland Run kicks off at ten and is due to pass the courthouse at twelve exactly. Once again—for the last time, I suddenly realize—I dress myself in the pink suit.

For my march to the gallows, Ginny chose her boldest accessories yet, dressing the suit down as a nod to the athletic nature of the event. Under the jacket I am wearing a cotton scoop-neck t-shirt, plastic wrist bangles, a broad-rimmed sunhat and running shoes, all in a matching shade of pink that is—unbelievably—even wilder and deeper and more outrageous than the suit itself. These accessories are not quite in the neon family—Ginny would never go that far—but they're damn close. She must have scoured the internet for weeks to find these items. I assemble the crazy getup and stare at myself in the mirror. The sight makes me conclude that the goal, according to Ginny and Ophelia and Jennifer, is to make me visible from space.

"Wow," says Tim. He'd awakened and was gazing at me with a smirk on his lips.

"Close your eyes," I say. "I don't want to blind you."

"Ah, but how lovely a last sight you would be," he says.

"I look like a Walmart birthday cake."

"Come here," says Tim. "Let me taste your frosting."

We arrive late to the Boland Run. I show up at the starting point with my suit in wrinkles, my eyeliner smeared, and a post-sex tangle of hair clumped at the back of my head.

Given the theatrics underway, my disheveled state goes unnoticed. The Fan Club has finally outdone itself. For one thing, they have multiplied; at least fifty of them are assembled behind the crowd of serious-looking runners. They have organized themselves into four tidy rows, looking very much like a military formation of a platoon of soldiers awaiting their command to march forward.

Except that they're wearing dyed pink long johns decorated with spiral lines curving around and around like a barbershop pole. And atop each of their heads is a huge, comically tall hat in the exact shade of my suit: Boland Pink. They look like Cats-in-the-Hat, except their hats are pointed at the tip.

"What the hell?" says Tim.

As we approach and the hats come more clearly into view, I understand what they've done. "Drill bits," I say. "Oh my god, they've dressed up as drill bits."

One of the pink bits dashes up to us, waving her arms and smiling. It's Jennifer. Up close, her costume is shockingly pink. "Thank God you're here," she squeals. "We were getting worried!" Across her chest in bright white are printed the words A BIT OF DEATH.

"I love you so much," I tell her, overcome by the sight of these volunteers, these crazies, these diehard defenders of democracy, reasonable people willing to make fools of themselves in these ridiculous costumes.

Jennifer grins like a little girl and leaps into the air. "Hooray!" she shrieks. "We were afraid you'd hate it."

"I do hate it," I say, laughing. "I hate it a lot."

Tim reaches out a hand and knocks on Jennifer's hat. "Sturdy," he says.

Jennifer indicates a woman passing through the ranks of the Fan Club, inspecting and adjusting costumes. Her chest blares A BIT OF CANCER. "Diana," she explains. "Costume director for the Greenville High drama department. She's a genius with papier mâché."

One by one the Fan Club turns, realizing I've arrived. They remain in formation, waving and calling out to me. One by one I recognize them: here's Phyllis, the blue haired lady-who-lunches, the friendliest and most reliable phone banker in the history of the Greenville Democratic Party. She waves frantically from her place in the formation. Her T-shirt reads A BIT OF LYING.

I see Jeremy, the bearded and skinny-jeaned twenty-year-old junior at the University of Greenville, political science major and diehard socialist with arms outstretched as if ready to give me one of his signature free hugs, standing in one of those silly pink swirly hats and wearing a T-shirt that reads A BIT OF DENIAL.

And there's my mother, facing me in determination, smiling, and weeping. Her shirt reads A BIT OF LOSS.

Jennifer directs me to the center of their ranks and they form a wide open square around me. We move forward, a coordinated bulk of bodies with me at the middle. I'm walking alone and yet surrounded by an army of smiling pink phalluses. This may be the strangest thing I've ever done. Given the looks on some of the faces of the drill bit soldiers marching alongside me, I'm not the only one who finds this scene surreal.

Ophelia has assured me I can expect the minimum sentence. I'll be given eighteen months, and in all likelihood I'll do twelve or fourteen. Because of the cancer, I'll be sent first to the new minimum security hospital the state has just opened, having privatized its construction and management to a private incarceration conglomerate.

I'm past the worst part of my treatment anyway. The chemo has done its work. Now, I'm thinking only as far as my recovery in the prison hospital. When the prison doctors have decided I'm well enough, I'll be transferred somewhere else for the duration of my sentence. Ophelia couldn't be sure where that might be. I'm trying not to think that far in advance.

I committed a felony. According to state statute, my career in politics is over. I suppose that's only right. It's hard to argue against laws keeping felons from holding public office. Then again, I think about my old friends who are felons because they laid down in front of bulldozers to protect forests or were caught bringing terrorized people across borders to safety. I wonder how different the world would be if they were the ones running things now. I think about July. I wonder where she is now and how she's doing.

But I'm not in jail yet. Right now, I'm surrounded by smiling, happy people wearing pink long johns and pointy Dr. Seuss hats. They're delightedly waving to the large crowd. Ahead of me I spot Dan, my loyal media guy, in a shirt that says A BIT OF SPIN, furiously thumbing his cell phone as he struggles to stay in formation. Behind Dan there's Manuel, my former strategy consultant. He spots his family on the sidelines and breaks ranks to sweep his delighted little girl off the curb and onto his shoulders. His shirt reads A BIT OF PROFIT. Evidently, the PR team has been busy. All of Greenville seems to be here.

We maintain a steady pace, past the high school and the drugstore and over the tracks toward downtown. I am aware of every step taking me closer to my punishment. From the corner of my eye, I find a familiar face. It's Mrs. Quinto, Mercedes' grandmother, wearing the pink costume with more dignity than one would think possible and a T-shirt that reads A BIT OF HUBRIS. She sees me looking her way and winks.

I feel a tug at my shoulder and there's Ginny, walking purposefully at my elbow. I feel her professional hand tuck the label of my blouse back into my collar. "For goodness sakes, Peg, must I *dress you*, too?" she whispers. I turn and behold her in a drill bit hat, customized in silk and feathers and pink long johns that could only have been cashmere. Her shirt reads A BIT OF BAD TASTE.

"Thank you, dearheart," I say.

"You look great in pink," she tells me. "And you know it." She falls back into her spot in the line.

Now the marching drill bits are carrying little pink flags with my face plastered in the middle of them. I find Jennifer in the crowd, looking at me and grimacing apologetically. *Yes*, I mouth to her. *I hate that a lot.* She's walking now between my mother and her mother. Poor Tina, she's doing a terrible job of looking cheerful in a shirt announcing A BIT OF PAIN.

When we pass the corner of Main Street and Greenville Boulevard, my eye drifts toward the little park bench by the ice cream shop, where Tina and Billy and I used to sit with our father licking ice cream cones after his union meetings. He always dragged us along to those general assemblies. He said we needed to hear how the world works. Plus, he bribed us with promises of ice cream afterward.

On the same bench, there sit my father and grandfather, and between them a ghostly version of my brother, clearly having a hard chemo day and too weak to stand. The crowd on the sidewalk opens up to allow the three of them a clear view of the procession coming by. They are surrounded by television cameras. I glance at Manuel and Dan, who are high-fiving and fist-pumping.

The three men are in their work clothes, long-faced. They wear their cobalt blue jumpsuits with yellow neon reflective armbands, dirty white helmets, and steel-toed work boots. The three of them sit on the park bench, ignoring the cameras and the crowd as though on a somber lunch break. Billy holds a cardboard sign on which are painted the words A BIT OF BETRAYAL.

The Fan Club goes silent as we pass. Then someone shouts, *Bravo, boys!* and a round of spontaneous applause breaks out for the Glass men.

The finish line is just still ahead, with its gauntlet of Boland Foundation dignitaries and corporate executives to be confronted.

As we approach the end point, the real potential for conflict occurs to me— everyone at the front of the race are die-hard Boland Foundation supporters. In order to get to my sentencing hearing, I'll need to walk straight into—and through—the enemy camp.

My army of pink-clad volunteers feels like insufficient protection. Did they realize how dicey things were about to get? Everyone around me is high on the applause and community love we've been shown along the route. I recognize in some of their eyes the glazed, addicted look of the political junkie.

The Fan Club, however, is astonishingly well-organized. Apparently, they held more than a few midnight practices in the plaza. The plan they rehearsed was to stand in a line at the far ends of the gathering—the speakers' podium would be inside the white pagoda at the center of the plaza—encircling the event nonviolently, quietly, and without confronting anyone.

Their comic costumes bearing tragic messages would stand in stark contrast to the unveiling of Regional Oil's pinkwashed bits. Behind them, onstage, would be the board of the Boland Foundation, their hands metaphorically dripping with suds. After a suitable few moments to let the imagery sink in, the drill bits would turn silently from the gathering and accompany me across the street to the courthouse for my sentencing.

This plan was modified in the final minutes, given that word of our coming had passed down the run route. In an attempt to take the wind out of our sails, the organizers began their wrap-up remarks fifteen minutes early. By the time we arrive, the pagoda is full of corporate reps and donors and politicians, facing the crowd. The Boland organizers have nearly succeeded in rushing through the script. Evidently they were hoping to put the crowd of supporters and donors in an admiring and grateful mood before we protesters arrived.

When the pink contingent arrives at the plaza, the CEO of Regional Oil, Sheila Maguire, is making her closing remarks onstage. At her elbow on a tasteful platform draped in white satin is displayed a single pink industrial drill bit. It looks like a terrible menacing sculpture. As my Fan Club and I linger in confusion at the back of the audience, the crowd is starting to turn in their seats to look at us. There we stand, a pink-suited politician and her fifty pink human drill bits, hesitating.

In street theater, timing is everything. We'd missed the beginning of the show, so improvisation is all we had left.

Beyond the stage, where Sheila Maguire now stands gulping at us nervously, the courthouse looms. I catch Jennifer's eye; we stride toward one another. "Go," I say, jerking my chin down the central aisle of the plaza, directly toward the podium. "I'll meet you at the courthouse. And take your time."

Jennifer pushes through to the front line and quickly organizes her drill bit army into pairs. Off they go, as slowly as a wedding procession, two by two down the aisle, splitting when they reach the stage and continuing on, soundlessly, toward the courthouse.

When the first of the drill bits comes floating down the aisle, Sheila Maguire remains standing at the podium. She tries to continue her remarks about the benefits of natural gas exploitation, but very quickly they sound hollow and unintentionally humorous, so she stops. So she stands silently, glaring at the spectacle. I've slipped around the edge of the crowd, watching her. She is gripping the edges of the podium in what can only be described as a barely controlled rage. Beside her, the attempt to dress up their own drill bit as an *objet d'art* looks suddenly idiotic.

Realizing she has utterly lost the attention of the crowd, Sheila Maguire is throwing a quiet little fit. She covers the microphone with her palm and through clenched teeth begins chewing out an associate. Finally as she raises her eyes to take in the length of the line of drill bits coming down the aisle, she abandons the podium. On her way past the drill bit pedestal, she gives it a vicious shove with her hip. The drill bit comes crashing to the stage with a crack as the wooden floorboards of the pagoda give way.

The television camera crews abandon the Boland Run for Cancer Research and follow us over to the courthouse. Ophelia by my side, I address the crowd, which has grown in size far beyond my fifty pink drill bits to include hundreds of people who joined the procession along the way. I say all the things I know how to say, all the things I've been saying to the cameras all along, and then I say a few more things, about what an honor it's been, about my hope for the future, etcetera. The Fan Club listens. The pointy tips of their drill hats glow in the sunshine like a range of pink mountains.

It's not as if my words are empty. It's just that I've said them a lot, over and over. I can fill the air with a lot of words. It's our specialty, we politicians. Our words save us from things we don't want to say. Things we don't want to admit. Questions we don't want to ask ourselves, such as whether we deserve what we're getting and whether we'd do it again. I don't have answers to either of those questions but I suspect I will by the time I'm out of this mess. Standing here on the courthouse steps moments before I'm to be carted off to prison, I speak and I speak. I mean what I say and the caring and brave people of Greenville listen and clap. They will go away feeling sad and wistful, glad it's me going to jail and not them, and I will go up the stairs to the courtroom and start serving my time in prison.

Ophelia taps my elbow. It's time to go. But I'm not ready. I keep talking. I keep telling them how much they mean to me, how much I've been moved by their stories. The woman activist with the dying chickens, and the man with the sick grandson, and the mother with the flaming tap water, and my dear dying brother. Bit by bit the people move closer to me. They take small tentative steps forward, getting close as if driven by the instinct for community.

In a moment this crowd will usher me gently into the courthouse. But right now, in my final moment of freedom, I notice how the noontime sunlight bounces off the crimson tile on the courthouse roof, bathing the plaza in rosy light. The Fan Club, my staff, my family, my constituents: everyone surrounds me, holding high those silly flags bearing my face. The sun shines through the fabric, washing me in pink.

Acknowledgements

My gratitude and thanks are extended to those individuals who helped me with their advice and encouragement. If anyone has been excluded from the list, it is clearly unintentional.

These people assisted me in every way possible, above and beyond the usual bonds of friendship, and I remain indebted for the continual kindness they showed me in making the book a reality: Shannon Cain, Mary Lawrence, Mary Ann Pressman, Gretchen Shine, Elizabeth Smith, Jessica Teal and Penny Waterstone.

Additionally, these individuals helped either by reading, editing, or just listening to me convey my thoughts and ideas: Garry Bryant, Jeannie Cooper, Karen Hla, Lisa Horwitch, Nance Crosby, Stephen Golden, Eve Hady, Martin Loy, Margy McGonagill, Arlene Mendez, Matt Messner, Berenice Milo, Stephanie A. Parker, Vera Pfeuffer, Marie Piccarreta, Barbara Sattler, Neil Sechan, Susan Tarrence, and Joshua Udovich.

And of course my two loving children, Brooke Sanders-Silverman and Adam Brent Silverman who are always there for me.